Winterfrost

Winterfrost

MICHELLE HOUTS

CANDLEWICK PRESS

Copyright © 2014 by Michelle Houts

First edition 2014

Library of Congress Catalog Card Number 2013955669
ISBN 978-0-7636-6565-4

14 15 16 17 18 19 BVG 10 9 8 7 6 5 4 3 2 1

Printed in Berryville, VA, U.S.A.

This book was typeset in Horley Old Style.

Candlewick Press
99 Dover Street
Somerville, Massachusetts 02144

visit us at www.candlewick.com

To the memory of Lene Bilslev-Jensen

Where dips the rocky highland

Of Sleuth Wood in the lake,

There lies a leafy island

Where flapping herons wake

The drowsy water rats;

There we've hid our faery vats,

Full of berrys

And of reddest stolen cherries.

Come away, O human child!

To the waters and the wild

With a faery, hand in hand,

For the world's more full of weeping than you can understand.

—from "The Stolen Child" by William Butler Yeats

Christmas Eve

From the outside looking in, it might have appeared to be an ordinary Christmas on the Larsen family's farm, nestled among the flat, snowy fields of an island called Lolland in the south of Denmark. The scent of kringle fresh from Mor's oven mingled with the woodsy smell of the wispy white pine that Far had brought indoors just hours before. Packages with neatly tucked corners and perfectly tied ribbons lay tempting beneath the tree.

Bettina Larsen secured small white candles to the tree's now-drooping boughs as little Christmas nisse decorations on the mantle conspired to lift her spirits. They tumbled and teased in their tiny brown coats and boots, their red stockings and pointed caps.

There was a fine duck roasting in the oven. There were family and friends and neighbors stopping by. Lively music filled the house as the Larsens circled the tree, hand in hand, their voices raised with songs the children learned early and the old would never forget. And despite the heaviness that weighed upon Bettina's heart this Christmas, there was a hint of a smile as she watched her baby sister twist herself up in ribbons and bows. What a gift baby Pia had been almost a year earlier, bringing new life to a home that had just said farewell to an old one.

Yes, it looked like an ordinary Christmas Eve, but it wasn't. Bettina wondered if there would ever be an ordinary Christmas without Farfar.

And then came the phone call. The phone call, which brought the news. The news, which was followed by the flurry of suitcases and last-minute instructions. *Feed the animals; keep the wood-fired furnace going; call if you need us. Everything will be just fine.*

It should have been an ordinary Christmas on the Larsen farm, nestled among the flat, snowy fields of an island called Lolland in the south of Denmark. But it wasn't. And if it had been, well, we wouldn't have much of a story to tell, now, would we?

Order

In spite of the chaos of the evening before, everything appeared to be going quite well the night after Christmas Eve. Bettina made a respectable supper for herself and baby Pia from holiday delicacies left from the previous day's celebration. She stacked the dishes neatly to dry after washing them—just as Mor would have done if she were there.

After supper Bettina took care to bundle Pia tightly before braving the bitter December air to feed the horses, goats, and chickens. In less than a week, the family would celebrate Pia's first birthday. There would be a big celebration with layer cake and neighbors and loved ones. Sorrow and joy played a game of tug-of-war inside Bettina's heart. This had always been Farfar's most beloved time of year. He loved Christmas, and he would have loved that Pia was born so close to his favorite holiday. Bettina remembered how he had taught her to fold red and white paper hearts when her tiny fingers were barely coordinated enough to crease the paper. He'd taken her to the barn and shown her how to twist slick yellow straw into sleek little *juleboker* or Christmas goats, with tightly braided horns. But in the year since Farfar had died, Bettina's joy for the holiday had disappeared, stored away inside her like the paper hearts and straw goats in the attic. Christmas at the Larsens' could never be the same without Farfar.

And yet time moved forward and, with or without Farfar, Christmas came as it always did. And Bettina had smiled. Some. And she had sung holiday songs. And to her surprise, she'd heard her own laugh when Pia had come downstairs in Mor's arms, dressed in a nisse costume, her right thumb in her mouth and left thumb in her ear. If ever there was a real-life nisse, Pia was it. Of course, nisse were among the many things that were debatably real in the life of a Danish twelve-year-old. But to Farfar, there had been no debate.

"The forests are full of tales unheard, if only humans would pause their busyness to listen," he would say, his voice thick with all the seriousness of a Sunday-morning vicar, but his eyes shining as bright as the eastern star. And never was Farfar as insistent about his beloved nisse as he was at Christmastime. "Although it's our holiday, not theirs, our wee friends delight in celebration, too," he would say. "Sure as I'm standing here, the nisse are out there, having their own Christmas party." And then he would turn his head to one side and listen, as if he could hear tiny nisse boots on the haymow floor while they danced and sang long into the night.

Farfar would have rejoiced in Pia's costume. He would have rejoiced in Pia, period. Everyone had said that it was tragic that little Pia would never know her grandfather, that she arrived not long after his passing. But Bettina had often wondered if they hadn't met somewhere in the place in between, her beloved grandfather and her new baby sister. She pictured a magical encounter, a tiny hand wrapped tightly around a wrinkled old finger for just a moment before one let go to glide gently toward the world the other had left behind. She never spoke of it. It sounded like something only a dreamer would imagine. It sounded like something Farfar would have believed.

And now Pia was nearly a year old, speaking a language only she could understand. And she was on the verge of walking—though still too young to be of any help with the chores.

Bettina shifted her sister on her hip and pulled a warm woolen hat snugly over the baby's blond curls before opening the door to the barn.

Felix, the Larsens' gray-blue hound, greeted them, leaping and tossing his body in circles with excitement.

"*Down!*" Bettina commanded, imitating Far's deep voice.

Felix jumped playfully at the girls, and when Bettina leaned down to scold him, he licked Pia's face and darted away before she had a chance to react.

"Oh, Pia!" Bettina cried. "I'm so sorry!"

But baby Pia didn't seem to mind the frantic dog's attention. She giggled and wiped her face with a pink-mittened hand.

Inside the barn, Bettina discovered her work was going to be more difficult than she had expected. She knew how to do the feeding. That wasn't the problem. Bettina had spent many an early morning and frosty evening helping Far. But carrying water and feed in buckets while keeping an eye on a baby — how would she hold her sister and carry a heavy bale of hay at the same time?

As she eyed the hay bales, Bettina came up with a plan. She quickly constructed a four-sided playpen of straw bales. Then she set her sister down in the middle. Little Pia's wide blue eyes peered up at her older sister with uncertainty. Soon enough a passing kitten caught her attention. The tubby orange tiger kitty first jumped up on the edge of a bale and then joined Pia inside the new play area. Pia squealed with delight, calling, *"Mee, mee!"* and Bettina set about her work in the barn.

The horses snorted impatiently as she dug into bags

of grain with the feed scoop. Their breath rose in puffs of white vapor from their wide, round nostrils and then quickly disappeared in the cold. Of all the animals in the barn, Bettina adored her father's horses most and gave them extra attention, stroking their velvety noses while she spoke first to Hans and then to Henrietta.

"You must be hungry. You're going to love this!"

Farfar could recall when horses were a necessary part of field work. But on a modern Danish farm, machinery had changed a horse's place from one of work to one of pleasure. And no one enjoyed the horses as much as Bettina. She had been saving for nearly a year to buy a horse of her own. Every bit of chore money or birthday money had gone into an empty Earl Grey tea tin that she kept hidden under her bed. Just last night she had slipped the Christmas money she'd gotten in a card from Aunt Inge into the tin and made a wish that it would never be used for anything other than her very own chestnut mare.

The goats were shoving and fighting for position in front of the feed bunk before Bettina even got around to breaking a bale of hay for them. She spoke to the noisy creatures with less affection than she had shown the horses. Even after they'd been fed, they seemed more interested in chewing Bettina's sleeves than the hay.

"Move over, you! Let go of that!" She pushed a big-bellied brown goat aside, but he came right back to chomp on her scarf. Bettina used her whole body to shove the nosy animal.

"Move out of my way!"

Finally, the goat gave up and turned his chewing attention to the wooden gate.

The chickens were the easiest to feed, as they were much less particular. Wherever their food landed, they would find it with their beaks, curved and sharp like the nose on a witch.

With the animals fed and watered, Bettina had only to stoke the fire in the big stove in the wood room, and then she and Pia could return to the house for the night. Like many old Danish farms, the Larsens' house and the barn sat next to each other. The house stood close to the road, and the red-brick barn stretched out the back toward the forest. Between the two, firewood filled a small room floor to ceiling. Far and their neighbor Rasmus Pedersen had spent months chopping wood, supplying the two families with ample fuel for the cold winter. A wood-burning stove warmed the home and kept the barn at a comfortable temperature for the animals, especially on cold Lolland nights.

Bettina gazed at the pile of wood. There was more than enough wood to keep the entire family warm until spring. Of course, Bettina's parents would be gone just a few days, not all winter. Far would be back in less than a week. And Mor had only taken the train as far as Århus.

Bettina's thoughts returned to Christmas Eve. The family had barely finished their meal of Christmas duck and rice pudding when the kitchen phone jingled. But instead of cheerful holiday greetings on the line, it was bad news. Mormor had fallen. She needed surgery on her hip. And with no one to sit with her at the hospital, decisions had to be made carefully and quickly. Mor would make the trip, stay until Mormor was released, and then bring her back to Lolland, where she could heal with the loving attention of her family.

Mor being gone a few days would have been no problem, except that Far was already planning to leave in the morning. Each year on Christmas Day,

Far journeyed to Skagen, at the northernmost tip of Denmark, to visit old Uncle Viggo. It wasn't exactly a trip he looked forward to, as Uncle Viggo was cranky and smoked the stinkiest of pipe tobaccos and rarely left his damp, musty cottage by the Kattegat Sea. But every year Far went for the week between Christmas and the new year. And every year he returned with enough tales of odd Uncle Viggo to entertain the family for weeks. Putting off the trip was not an option. Uncle Viggo would have thrown a conniption that could have been heard all the way to Sweden.

"A hospital and a stuffy old cottage are no place for a baby," Mor had fretted.

"Bettina can handle the barn chores and taking care of Pia," Far had said matter-of-factly. "After all, Pia's hardly an infant. And Bettina cares for her every day. Besides, the Pedersens are right next door if the girls need anything."

Mor looked uncertain, but when Far added, "Isn't that right, Bettina?" Bettina spoke right up.

"Of course. I'll take care of everything." It was a great

deal of responsibility, but Bettina was undaunted. She was, after all, the mature and responsible older sister.

Mor was still a bit hesitant, but Far's certainty and Bettina's confidence eased her worries. While the situation wasn't ideal, it was the best the family could do on such short notice. Bettina was quite capable, and the Pedersens next door would look in on the girls regularly. Besides, nothing ever happened on the sleepy island of Lolland in the dead of winter. What could possibly go wrong?

As Bettina stuffed the firebox full of wood, the heat from the fire rose and warmed her frosty cheeks. Another kind of warmth swelled deep beneath her coat and layers of clothing. It was pride. She had taken care of the meal, the house, the animals, the fire, and baby Pia. If she'd had any worries of being alone and in charge (which she didn't), they would have melted away like chocolate left too near the fire.

Yes, everything appeared to be perfectly in order on that Christmas night. Mor was taking care of Mormor, whose hip would heal with time. Far was off to appease a lonely and demanding old uncle. And Bettina was putting her baby sister to bed and turning out the last light in the red-brick house on the Larsen farm. Everything appeared to be just fine.

But something was out of order.

In their haste over the holiday meal, in their rush to get Mor and Far on their way, in their concern for Mormor, the Larsens had forgotten one very important Christmas tradition. And someone close by was not very happy at all.

Forgotten

Young Klakke peered out from a small crack in the hayloft window, not daring to move and hardly daring to breathe. What was happening with the Larsens? He simply had to know—even though it was nearly daylight and, under normal circumstances, he would have been well out of sight. But today's circumstances were anything but normal. And his curiosity proved stronger than any warnings that Gammel had tried to instill in his young mind about the dangers of breaking the rules.

Klakke opened the window just a smidge wider. Why were the Larsens gathering in the barnyard at this odd hour? He scooched forward for a closer look.

Watching the Larsens was not a new pastime for Klakke. In fact, it wasn't a pastime at all. It was his job. The family had been his responsibility for years now. And though he spent his nights trekking about in the forest, he was usually asleep in the highest part of the Larsens' barn long before the sun crept up over the frozen fields of Lolland. This was his place. His home. He looked after the family and the animals, doing what little kindnesses he could for such a small being.

And the Larsens? Well, they had always been quite kind to Klakke as well, though they knew very little of his existence. They had never seen him. And they certainly didn't know his name, which was as it should be.

Klakke knew some of the Larsens believed in nisse. The children always believed. Until a certain age, anyway. And the old grandfather had undoubtedly known Klakke was there. But the younger Mr. Larsen and his wife? And the girl Bettina? Klakke couldn't be sure about them, but he knew one thing to be true—Mr.

Larsen was no fool. A Danish farmer with any sense at all would do well to recognize that his barn *could* be home to a nisse, and should that be the case, he'd best stay on the nisse's good side.

Klakke knew he should have been deep in the cover of the hayloft on this Christmas morning. But at the tender age of sixty-two, Klakke was a young nisse and his sense of curiosity overpowered what little common sense he'd managed to store up. At the moment, he was glued to the crack in the hayloft window. His plump little fingers held it open just enough to see the family in the barnyard below.

The older Larsen girl, Bettina, stood in the doorway of the house with the little one they called Pia. Both waved as their mother and father left the driveway in the family's small red car and headed toward town. Klakke was clever and observant, and when he saw the large suitcases they took along, he quickly deduced that Mr. and Mrs. Larsen would be away for more than a day.

The door of the house closed, and the Larsen sisters disappeared inside. Klakke let the hayloft window close, too. There was nothing more to see out there.

Klakke wished he could venture out to tell Gammel about the Larsens; perhaps Gammel could explain why the Larsen parents were acting so strangely. But he dared not go where he might be seen. So Klakke settled into the straw feeling very unsettled and also very hungry.

For the Larsens had neglected their nisse last night. Christmas Eve, the one night each year when all Danish families—believers and unbelievers alike—acknowledge even the *possibility* of a nisse by placing a bowl of warm, bubbly rice pudding in the barn after the holiday meal. That small gesture was all it would take to appease their nisse friend for another year. And every year, without fail, the Larsens had left the bowl of pudding in the barn, topped with a nice clump of golden butter—because melted butter pleases a nisse more than just about anything.

Klakke remembered how Bettina had hollered with delight in years past when she found the empty bowl in the mow the next morning, every buttery drop of pudding licked clean. He scoffed at the adults who rationalized among themselves that the pudding had been devoured by hungry barn cats. But the young and the wise knew differently. To them, it was more than a holiday ritual—it was a time-honored fact. *Take care of your nisse, and your nisse will take care of you.*

The Larsens had never strayed from tradition. Not once had Klakke been overlooked on Christmas Eve.

Until now.

For the first time in twelve years, Klakke questioned having left his home in Falster, his parents, and his beloved twin sister, Klara, to come to the Larsen farm. Had he left his family only to be forgotten by the Larsens?

Klakke grumbled as a barn cat hopped up into the hayloft and stopped to look at him, as if wondering why he hadn't crawled into his bed of straw to disappear for the day. The mother cat, whose tail had been tugged a time or two by the mischievous nisse, had learned to be cautious. Taking her chances, she meandered over to Klakke and rubbed her chin against his small booted foot.

Klakke wasn't in any mood to play. He waited until the friendly feline was right on top of his boot, and then he flung the startled cat forward. She flew several feet and then landed, as always, on all fours, offended but unharmed. She gave Klakke a sideways glance and then disappeared over the edge of the mow floor to the safety of the barn below.

Winterfrost

Bettina woke the next morning in the upstairs bedroom that she shared with her sister still feeling groggy, even though she had slept the night through without waking once. She lifted her heavy head from her fluffy pillow and struggled to open her eyes. Had she slept so soundly that she'd missed her sister's occasional whimpers in the night? Or had Pia slept so soundly that she'd made not a single peep?

The bright winter daylight seeped in from behind the window shade and startled Bettina. She sat up quickly, trying to shake the fog from her brain. So much light could only mean it was well into the morning hours. The fire must surely have burned itself out.

And what about Pia?

Bettina's bare toes touched the wooden floor, and she was surprised to find it warm. The house wasn't cold at all. She hurried to the crib, where Pia, still sleeping, made a soft sighing sound before rolling to one side. Without even opening her eyes, Pia reached for her ever-present stuffed white goose, pulled it close, and settled back into a soft and peaceful slumber.

Bettina let out a relieved breath. Pia was fine. Across the room her own bed, still radiating the warmth of her body, called to her, promising sweet dreams. But as much as Bettina would have loved to crawl back into bed and disappear for the day, she knew she had responsibilities. Her parents were counting on her.

Without taking time to dress, Bettina went downstairs to check the fire. She could feel its warmth even as she opened the kitchen door and stepped into the wood room. Strangely, it had burned down only a little since she'd filled the firebox before going to bed the night before. Someone must have stoked the fire in the early morning hours. But who?

The answer, when it came to her, seemed obvious: Mr. Pedersen must have stopped by to check on them, knowing they were on their own. Likely he had entered the wood room to knock on the kitchen door, as neighbors never use front doors when visiting. When he hadn't gotten any answer, he had rightly assumed that the girls were still sleeping, and, like any good neighbor, he had added enough wood to keep the house warm until Bettina woke.

Bettina felt both secure and embarrassed at the same time. It was a comfort knowing that the Pedersens were close by. Rasmus and Lisa Pedersen would do just about anything for their neighbors. But at the same time, it annoyed her that on her first morning alone, she had not only slept late, but she had nearly let the house get cold in the dead of winter. So much for proving that she could handle the farm on her own!

Then Bettina had a thought. What if Mr. Pedersen felt like he needed to take care of the barn chores for her as well? She couldn't let that happen!

Still in her nightgown, Bettina threw a blanket over her shoulders and braced herself for the cold winter blast before opening the door.

When she pulled open the heavy oak door, she gasped—but it wasn't the cold air that stole the very breath from her lungs. An unexpected winter wonderland was laid out before her. Everything was white, from the fir trees to the red-brick barn to the thin fence wires. But it wasn't snow.

"Winterfrost!" Bettina cried.

Sometime after she and baby Pia had settled in for the night, a thick fog must have settled over Lolland, and as the night temperatures dipped, that fog had frozen itself to every blade of grass, every twig in the trees, leaving behind a thick sugary cover and air as still as a baby's breath. A winterfrost on Lolland was rare and spectacular, and Bettina could not recall the last time she'd seen such beauty. She barely felt a chill as she stood with the door open wide, staring at Mor's winter flower beds, now looking as though someone had sprinkled sparkly white sugar on every leaf and stem.

She wished Farfar could see this.

"There's nothing so wonder-filled as winterfrost. It's *magical!*" he would say, and Mor would scoff.

"What? You've heard the tales of winterfrost," he'd answer Mor. "The most mysterious of events occur during winterfrost."

"Tales, indeed! Fairy tales, I'd say!" Mor would press her lips together and shake her head. "Don't you go filling my girl's head with nonsense!"

But when Mor was out of earshot or when Farfar and Bettina walked alone in the woods, he spoke of winterfrost as if it were a magical doorway to another world. A rare and precious opportunity, afforded to those who believed in the goodness of nature and the possibility that we share the forest with more than just the animals who scurry across our boot-worn paths.

And now it was here, right before her eyes—a winterfrost! Bettina vowed to ride her bicycle to the churchyard in town to tell Farfar about this day as soon as Mor or Far returned home.

A soft sound from above pulled Bettina's thoughts back into the house. Pia was awake and needed her. Bettina quickly closed the door and threw the blanket over a peg on the wall. She raced up the narrow wooden stairs, eager for her baby sister to experience this fantastic winter phenomenon for the very first time, and thrilled to be the one who would get to show it to her.

"Pia," she called on the way up, "wait until you see what's outside!"

But in all her excitement over the winterfrost, Bettina had neglected to notice one thing. There were no tracks in the snow in the driveway, nor were there any on the walk leading to the house. Mr. Pedersen had not been there that morning.

Mischief

Klakke spent his night traveling between the barn and the forest, his mood sour. He didn't go see Gammel, mostly because Gammel would know that Klakke had been up to no good. And he'd know without Klakke saying a word, for many an old nisse could look directly inside the heart of another. And no one had mastered that skill as well as Gammel.

At some time in the night, under the cover of darkness, Klakke had returned to the barn, his pockets full of herbs and his mind filled with mischief. The large red

barn door was closed, but Klakke had no trouble pushing it open just a crack; like all nisse, he was especially
strong for his size. This time he didn't bother to close
the door behind him.

Hans and Henrietta were pawing at their stall doors,
and both gave a loud whinny when they saw their small
friend. Most times Klakke would have returned the
friendly *hello*s, but not this night. Tonight the little nisse
only scowled at the horses. He did what he'd come to do,
then climbed the ladder swiftly in spite of the fact that
it was quite obviously made for legs much longer than
his own.

Klakke tried, but he couldn't sleep. It wasn't morning
yet, and his body's clock was telling him he ought to be
in the forest visiting with the night animals. Or gathering nuts for his daytime friends. But a strange sadness
that very much resembled self-pity had settled so deep
into his bones, he was sure they ached.

The little nisse sighed and peered out of the loft's
only window and into the early morning darkness. In
the light of the farm's single barnyard lamp, he could
see that a heavy fog had come down like a fluffy white

blanket over everything, hiding from view the ground below. A fog so dense on a cold night like this just might bring . . .

For the first time since Christmas Eve, Klakke's heavy heart lightened a bit. He flew out of the hayloft with such quickness, the sleepy barn cats didn't even have time to be startled. He had to get outdoors and see for himself.

Hans and Henrietta eyed the nisse suspiciously, but Klakke didn't bother to stop. He squeezed himself through the crack in the red wooden barn door, and there it was.

A winterfrost!

Young Klakke had experienced only a handful of winterfrosts in his lifetime, and each one he found to be more fascinating than the last. He was almost giddy with excitement as he skipped around the barnyard. Then he slowed to a walk, mesmerized by the crystals of frozen fog around him.

The small fir seedlings at the forest's edge, barely taller than he, wore furry winter coats of white. The grasses drooped low to the ground with their load of fluffy frost. The air was still and silent. Even the Baltic breeze held its breath as if it were trying not to disturb the delicate balancing act that nature had accomplished overnight.

Klakke didn't want to go back to the barn, but the morning sky was pinking up on the horizon. Daylight was coming, and, especially in the great whiteness that surrounded him, it would be impossible to stay hidden in his brown coat, red stockings, and red hat.

It was an age-old dilemma of the nisse: how to dress in such a way that they might be unseen by human eyes, yet conspicuous enough to the hawk so as not to be mistaken for a rabbit running across the fields of grass. The red hats gave birds of prey plenty of notice that a nisse was not dinner to be snatched up and carried away, but it made them more likely to be spotted by humans. However, thanks to toes turned slightly inward, nisse can run so fast that they're out of sight before the human brain even has time to register what the eyes saw—or thought they saw. No opportunities for double takes. When a nisse is gone, he's gone.

With daylight creeping across the island, Klakke

reluctantly returned home, climbed the ladder, and tried to sleep. But he didn't sleep well. Below he could hear Bettina's soft voice as she spoke kindly to the animals (except the goats—everyone, even Bettina, always spoke firmly to the naughty goats) while doing the morning chores.

Soon she would discover Klakke's pranks. But why should this interrupt his daily slumber? After all, he'd been mischievous but not mean. His pranks had caused no real harm.

Still, he felt the need to see Bettina's expression when his mischief was discovered. Soundlessly he crawled to the edge of the mow and peered below.

Something in the Air

"You play with the kitties while I get to work," Bettina told Pia. "This won't take long at all. Then we can take a walk in the forest. You've never seen the forest in a winterfrost."

But the feeding took longer than ever. First, Bettina reached for the horse feed, but it wasn't where it normally was. After a quick search, she found it sitting where the chicken feed usually sat.

"How strange," she muttered to herself. "That isn't where I left the horse feed."

Bettina moved the bags back to their proper positions and then reached for a feed scoop hanging on the wall.

"What in the world?" Bettina asked aloud. Where three metal feed scoops usually hung on the barn wall, there were three empty hooks. She put her hands on her hips and turned to look around. She spotted the scoops hanging from three hooks that usually held the broom, shovel, and pitchfork.

"Now, where are *they*?"

Pia babbled something Bettina didn't understand. The little girl's eyes were fixed on the hayloft, and she giggled with delight.

But Bettina wasn't delighted. She was beginning to grow less annoyed and more uncomfortable. How had everything become so mixed up overnight? Bettina shook off a shiver and spoke to Pia in a cheerful voice.

"My goodness, Pia. I need to do a better job putting my tools away from now on."

Before long, Bettina spotted the missing shovel, broom, and pitchfork lying haphazardly in a pile of loose straw. She put everything back in its place.

She fed Hans and Henrietta and then moved on to the

noisy goats. The goats seemed agitated, although they were rarely calm. But today their throaty *maaaaaa*s were louder than ever. All three jumped up, front hooves on the gate, *maaaa*-ing wildly as Bettina passed by.

"Settle down, you!" she commanded. She patted their necks and gently lifted their bony legs off the gate. Their chaos quieted to small grunts.

But when Bettina lifted the goats' feed buckets from their pen, she saw that all the buckets were as full as they'd been the night before. No wonder the goats were acting crazy! They hadn't eaten even a bite of feed!

"What's the matter, guys? Aren't you feeling well?"

The goats still seemed anxious, but their eyes were bright and they appeared healthy. Hungry, yes, but they didn't look sick. The grain must be the problem. If Far were there, Bettina thought, he'd tell her to dump it and replace it with fresh rations. So that's exactly what she planned to do, although not without a twinge of guilt. It wasn't in the nature of any good Danish farmer to waste anything.

In a moment of compromise that Bettina decided was nothing short of brilliant, she took the grain outside and scattered it behind the barn where the forest bordered Mor's gardens and the smallest of the wild animals often came to nibble. Surely the rabbits, birds, and squirrels would consider the oats and molasses a wonderful find when they happened upon them in the snow. Bettina was feeling quite pleased with herself as she watched the grain fall like confetti on the frosty ground. As she did, the faint smell of something familiar wafted through the air and caught her quite by surprise. What *was* that smell?

Mixed with the scents of molasses and oats was an odor that brought to mind a warm kitchen and Mor's creamed potatoes next to a beautifully baked leg of lamb, steaming from the oven. Rosemary! That was the smell—fresh and green. She was sure of it. The goats' feed smelled distinctly of rosemary!

All at once some things became much clearer to Bettina—and others made less sense than before. She knew why the goats hadn't eaten. They hated the smell and taste of rosemary. Bettina was certain of this because one day last summer they had found a way out of their pen and into the herb garden, where they had chewed every last plant down to the bare roots in the soil. Every last plant *except* the rosemary, which was left standing tall all by itself in the garden. Bettina would never forget Mor's frustration. "Our herb garden!" she had grumbled. "Those horrible beasts!"

But knowing *why* the goats hadn't eaten brought little comfort to Bettina's troubled thoughts. How had something so odd gotten into the feed? Fresh rosemary didn't grow in the garden in the dead of winter. It wasn't even something that was kept in the barn. Someone had to have mixed it in with the oats. But who? Who could have — who *would* have — come into the barn in the night?

Bettina filled the goats' feed buckets with fresh grain, but not before taking a good whiff just to be sure. Nothing unusual. Just goat feed.

Baby Pia stood at the edge of the straw playpen and babbled wordlessly toward the hayloft as her sister finished the chores. As soon as the animals were fed, Bettina didn't waste any time. She snatched up her baby sister and whisked her off into the house. She would have to introduce Pia to the winterfrost later.

The truth was, Bettina didn't like being in the barn anymore. She didn't like that she felt wary of every creak and groan in the rafters. And she especially didn't like the strange nagging feeling in the back of her neck, the feeling that someone was watching her every move.

Winter Nap

Inside the Larsens' cozy home, baby Pia played with her dolls on the carpet until her contented coos turned to pouts for Bettina's attention. Soon pouting turned to short bouts of fussiness, and when Pia rubbed her eyes with two chubby fists, Bettina knew. It was time to nap. Putting her sister down to sleep was a task Bettina had done for Mor many times. There was a sort of routine involved, and Bettina knew just how to go about it.

First, she gathered Pia's pink cotton blanket and the well-worn stuffed goose from the crib upstairs. Then

Bettina scooped up her baby sister, who was now yawning deeply. Finally, the pair settled into Mor's wooden rocking chair, and Bettina sang softly and clearly while they rocked.

"Solen er så rød, mor,
og skoven blir så sort . . ."

It was a nighttime song about the sun setting red in the sky and the forest becoming dark, and of all the Danish lullabies, it was Bettina's favorite. She couldn't say she actually remembered Mor singing it to her, but when Mor sang it to Pia, she felt a calm deep in her bones that could only come from having heard the same soothing melody when she was a baby. Now, as Bettina sat rocking and singing to Pia, she felt the child's body slowly relax and then melt comfortably into her lap. Before the third verse was finished, Pia was sleeping soundly.

Just to be certain, Bettina repeated the lullaby once more, then rose slowly and cautiously, watching Pia's face with every step. Bettina relaxed a little when Pia didn't move a muscle. The child was fast asleep. Bettina carried her sister to the pram that sat waiting by the back door. Inside the little carriage, Pia's bunting was open and ready for Bettina to lay the baby inside. Pia sighed softly and turned her face to snuggle in the warmth of the bunting, but her eyelids never fluttered. Bettina tucked a thick wool blanket around all sides of the pram and then draped one final layer over the top before opening the back door. She wheeled the carriage outside and, just as Mor would have done, positioned the pram where she could see it clearly from the kitchen window.

"Children need fresh air," Mormor would say, and every Danish mother and grandmother would agree. Rain or shine, winterfrost or no winterfrost, Danish babes must be set outside to nap. Only the harshest of weather conditions, say a thunderstorm or a blizzard, would keep the sleeping children indoors.

Being out in the winterfrost once again filled Bettina with wonder. She lingered long enough to appreciate how each pine needle seemed to sport its own feathery white coat. But Bettina was not dressed for the out-doors like Pia, and she shivered in the damp stillness. She returned to the house, leaving her sister to take in as much fresh air and as many sweet dreams as a baby could possibly absorb in one afternoon.

Inside, Bettina made herself a cup of tea, which was really a cup of hot water, a small amount of tea, and a heaping scoop of honey. If Mor had been home, she would have scolded Bettina for taking so much honey. But Mor wasn't home, and after successfully getting Pia down for her nap, Bettina was feeling very grown-up and felt she could decide for herself how much honey to put in her tea.

She settled on the sofa near the picture window, where she had a clear view of Pia's pram but not much else. The fog that had created the winterfrost had not lifted, and even the Pedersens' farm was lost in the haze. Somewhere the snowy fields met the gray-white sky, but the line between the two smeared like a wet paint-ing hung too soon. The frosted treetops of the forest blended so perfectly with the low-hanging clouds that they, too, seemed to have become one. Bettina rested her head against the sofa cushions and stared out into the whiteness that Lolland had become.

She thought of Mormor and her broken hip in Århus. Mor had reached her by now. She thought of the goats and then of the tiny forest animals, and she wondered if they had found the grain behind the barn. She gazed at the white landscape and imagined two gray rabbits coming upon the oats and nibbling contentedly on the newfound treat.

Within minutes Bettina's eyes closed, and Lolland disappeared.

For the second time in a single day, Bettina woke from a deep sleep feeling confused and a bit uncertain. How long had she been asleep? A quick glance out the window told her that Pia's carriage was still outdoors and the blankets around the little girl hadn't moved at all. Bettina turned on a light, and the dusky room filled with a warm glow, urging Bettina toward a more coherent frame of mind. It was time to wake Pia and begin dinner preparations. Bettina took her now-cold tea to the kitchen and opened the door to the back garden.

She pulled baby Pia's carriage back into the house and shut the door.

"Time to wake up, little one," Bettina cooed, removing the warm pink drape from the pram. When she did, she gasped and her hands flew to her mouth.

Baby Pia was gone.

Restless

That very afternoon, high in the hayloft, Klakke wasn't sleeping well at all. Nothing had gone as he wished these past two days. He'd not yet forgiven the Larsens for their neglect. He'd had his nisse revenge, but messing up the barn and tampering with goat feed hadn't brought him the satisfaction he'd expected. Klakke liked Bettina, and her uneasiness in the barn only brought regret to the young nisse.

Even the winterfrost hadn't completely lifted his spirits. Stuck in the barn until dark, he was certain that at any moment the sun would come along and burn its way through the clouds. If that happened, the fog would be gone, taking the beautiful winterfrost with it. And no one could say when another would come.

For hours Klakke tossed and turned and dreamed, until at last he woke, curious to see if the wonderful winter landscape remained. It was not yet dusk. Common sense told him to stay hidden, but once again his youthful impulses won out.

Outside, Klakke was pleased to find that the sun had stayed behind the clouds the entire day. The winterfrost had survived! Slowly, Klakke felt his grudge against the Larsens fade. He was beginning to feel like his old cheerful self again. Klakke darted across the all-white barnyard to the forest's edge, whistling and kicking up his feet as he went. He still didn't understand why the Larsens would neglect to leave his rice pudding on Christmas Eve, but in the still beauty of the winterfrost, Klakke's anger cooled and he was able to think clearly. The awful oversight likely had something to do with Mr. and Mrs. Larsen leaving in a hurry. Perhaps the family had been too distracted to remember their poor nisse. Well, he could forgive them just this once. He knew that Gammel would say that forgiveness is the kindest of paths to take. Klakke was finished with his tricks. He was ready to behave himself again.

By the time Klakke finished parading around the farm, he found himself at the edge of the Larsens' back garden. It was late afternoon, pushing evening, and there were no lights on in the house.

Curiosity pulled him into the Larsens' garden, where in the summer he loved to gaze at the beautiful flower beds, but where he seldom dared to go. What if some-one was looking out from the big windows in the brick house?

In a particularly bold move, Klakke ventured through the neatly trimmed hedges, now heavy with frost. He took a cobblestone path from the garden shed to the back patio, where he only hesitated a moment before climbing two small stone steps. He realized that he was closer to the house than he'd ever been before, but a deep sense of wonder drove him on, toward something on the patio that he'd seen often.

He never could say exactly why he did it. It wasn't

an act of revenge, for he really had forgiven the Larsens for their neglect. Rather, the winterfrost seemed to have a strange effect on the mischievous little nisse, pushing him toward the house, toward the pram, and right up to baby Pia.

Klakke climbed up the side of the pram without jarring it at all. When his eyes fell upon little Pia, he drew in his breath in both wonder and awe. The human baby was sleeping like a snow angel, so sweet and innocent. Her round pink cheeks puffed out with each breath.

And then, although he didn't set out that December afternoon to do what he did, he lifted her gently from the pram.

And Klakke stole baby Pia.

Panic

Bettina stood only a moment in stunned silence before she ran back outdoors. *Pia could not have gone far,* she thought. Bettina was clearly flustered and not thinking rationally. For if she had been, she would have realized that Pia could not have gone anywhere at all. The child couldn't even walk.

Bettina's mind and heart seemed to be in a race against one another, both pounding so crazily it felt as if an undirected orchestra had taken residence inside of her. Her stockinged feet responded to the awful music as she darted aimlessly about the patio and garden in search of her baby sister. Gradually, logic prevailed. There was no way Pia could have climbed out of her carriage and wandered away on her own. And then a thought like the dull thud of a bass drum brought the music to a sudden halt: *If Pia didn't leave on her own, someone must have taken her!*

Like the steady, unstoppable evening shadows in the forest, panic set in. Bettina searched the frosty patio for footprints and found none besides her own frantic tracks heading here and there and in circles. Anyone taking the baby from the pram would have left tracks. It made no sense at all. What was she missing?

Bettina's eyes darted around the garden. In all directions, the delicate winterfrost appeared undisturbed. Not a branch or a twig had been shaken.

Bettina was just about to search the barn when she noticed a small spot near the stone path that led into the forest — a spot that appeared darker, less sparkly than its surroundings. She followed the path and examined the area closely. The seedlings that grew low at the edge of the forest were bare. Something had knocked all the frost off the tiny branches. And yet there were no footprints, no other clues to follow. She eyed the patio and let her eyes follow the path to the place she knelt. What was small enough to disturb only the tiniest branches but large enough to carry off a baby — all without leaving footprints in the snow? Some sort of bird? An animal that could hop great distances?

But no such creatures existed in the forests of Denmark — or anywhere else that Bettina knew of.

Barely able to breathe, Bettina stood and faced the forest.

"Pia!" she called, but only her trembling voice came back from the darkness, sounding emptier and lonelier than when it had left her throat.

Perhaps a strong wind had lifted the baby from her pram, Bettina thought crazily. *Perhaps Pia was just out of sight, shivering and cold, but unharmed under the cover of the pines.* Bettina stepped cautiously forward, her socks now soaked and her toes so cold she could no longer feel them.

But what was a dusky evening in the garden was black as midnight under the trees.

"Solen er så rød, mor,
og skoven blir så sort . . ."

The lullaby Bettina had sung earlier that day floated through her mind.

"The sun is so red, mother,
the forest is so black . . ."

"PIA!" Bettina shouted once more, but the dark trees answered with silence. Bettina shivered. She wasn't dressed to be so long outdoors. Her toes ached. She had to get inside.

All across Lolland, the winterfrost remained, but without the daylight, it had lost its sparkle. As Bettina eyed the empty baby carriage in the kitchen, she couldn't help but hear Farfar's voice.

The most mysterious of events occur during winterfrost.

Search

Bettina raced to put on heavy clothes — snow pants, a down-filled ski jacket. On a shelf by the door, she found Far's warmest gloves and, in the wood room, her own snow boots. So what if it was dark? She told herself she wasn't scared of the dark or of the forest or of strange and mysterious happenings. A younger Bettina might have been afraid, but this Bettina was old enough to be left in charge. Finding Pia was her job. As she dressed, she formed and re-formed a plan in her head.

Her first idea had been to contact Mor or Far, but she quickly thought better of that. They were a long way from Lolland, and what could they do except worry? Worry and be disappointed that Bettina had been unable to handle the responsibilities they'd asked of her.

Instead, Bettina would enlist the Pedersens' help. Her parents had told her to call the Pedersens if anything went wrong. She ran to the kitchen and grabbed the telephone. Three times, six times, eight times the phone rang in her ear, and no one picked up at the Pedersens'.

Bettina hurried to the window that looked out across the empty fields toward the neighboring farm. Through the foggy twilight, she could see that not a single light glowed in the Pedersens' house or barn. And their pickup truck wasn't in the driveway.

The Pedersens were not home.

There was only one thing left to do. Bettina went back outside and headed straight to the edge of the forest. It was a vast expanse of trees, stretching from one side of the island to the other. Massive oaks and tall pines intermingled, forming a dense wood interrupted only by the clearing where Far and Mr. Pedersen cut their firewood. Though void of large trees, the area was dense with scrub brush and newly planted seedlings.

Bettina surveyed the dark woods before her. Within these shadowy depths was a path that she knew well. One direction headed toward town, while the other wound through acres and acres of forest before it eventually led to the sea. No sooner had Bettina started down the path than she wished she had thought to bring a flashlight. The evening was dark, but inside the forest it was black.

She glanced nervously to one side and then the other. It was the same forest where the birds sang sweetly and the woods' flowers bloomed all summer, she told herself. But at night, in the dead of winter, the forest whispered unfriendly thoughts. Birds lurked, nesting above her head, and squirrels and mice shot out unexpectedly across the dark path. What other creatures might be hiding just out of sight? Bettina closed her ears and her mind to everything except finding Pia and walked on.

Far had shown her years ago how to follow tracks in the snow, so Bettina kept her eyes on the forest floor. But much to her dismay, the only tracks in the woods were her own. It appeared that no one else had traveled this way since the last snowfall.

Still, she continued on. She stepped gingerly at first, unsure of what was hidden beneath the coating of frost and snow. With deliberate steps, she tried to land squarely on solid ground, but occasionally she stepped on a fallen branch or a small log and nearly lost her balance. Long spindly branches reached out from the dense underbrush, snagging her coat and tugging at her as she walked. Bettina tried to keep her thoughts focused firmly on her mission, but stories of witches and ghosts and trees that suddenly come to life and grab young girls were never far from her mind.

It was pitch-dark now, the sky above the woods no longer distinguishable from the branches. What help would she be to Pia if she got lost in the woods overnight? Bettina had no choice but to retrace her quickly fading footsteps to the place where the forest met the garden path leading directly to her own backyard.

Reluctantly, she followed the path all the way to her back door. Someone had been on the patio and taken Pia. But who? No one could have done it without leaving footprints, she reasoned. Everyone — every*thing* — leaves footprints.

Everything but ghosts and spirits and nisse.

Bettina was quite sure that she didn't believe in ghosts and spirits. But nisse? She had once been a believer. But as a person grew, logic had a way of prevailing over magic, and Bettina's childish certainty had faded. But Farfar's belief had never waned. He had been as certain of nisse as he was of the hair on his head.

Bettina stood, wide-eyed at the thoughts that tumbled inside her mind. Was it possible? Mor and Far would shake their heads and scoff at the notion. But with Pia missing, Bettina could rule nothing out.

If there were such things as nisse, she decided, and *if* one lived on the Larsens' farm, then there was only one place for her to go next.

She ran to the barn. Bursting through the door, she flipped on the lights and yelled, "My name is Bettina Larsen, and I want my sister back!"

Hans and Henrietta raised their heads from their feed buckets and stopped chewing. The goats stared, and the barn cats backed away from Bettina's unexpected outburst. There was silence.

Bettina stood frozen. Her eyes were on the mow

above, and her ears strained, listening for any small noise. There was nothing.

"Listen here, nisse," she shouted into the air, dismayed at the lack of authority in her voice. She cleared her throat and continued. "If you are here and if you took my sister, I want you to bring her back to me tonight!"

There was still no reply. Bettina turned to go. Hans and Henrietta had once again stuck their heads in their grain buckets and resumed their noisy munching, but otherwise all was still. Bettina stopped in her tracks. Noisy munching? She hadn't done the evening feeding yet.

Bettina looked around. The horses had fresh grain. The goats stood with hay hanging from each side of their mouths. Water buckets were filled to the brim with cold, clear water. Even the cats' feed pan was topped off.

If she'd had any doubts at all about whether or not there was a nisse in the Larsens' barn, they were quickly subsiding. But who was this nisse? And, more importantly, was he there to help or to harm?

Epiphany

Panic and determination faded into desperation. If only she hadn't slept while Pia napped! Surely the nisse wouldn't have dared to take Pia if Bettina had been watching her. But why would a nisse want a baby? No answer Bettina could imagine made her feel any better.

Inside the kitchen, Bettina turned on the lights. There sat Pia's pram, just as Bettina had left it. What if the past hours had been nothing more than a bad dream? What if Pia had been there sleeping all along? With a small glimmer of hope—and desperately in need of a miracle—Bettina approached the carriage and carefully moved the blankets. There was no sleeping baby. Only a well-worn stuffed goose. Pia had not been magically returned to her rightful place.

At once all the tears Bettina had been holding in came rushing out. She picked up the stuffed animal and held it to her face. It smelled sweet and fresh, like Pia after her bath. Bettina's heart ached. Where could Pia be on this cold night?

Bettina had been able to hold down the farm for just one and a half days before she let something so horrible happen. Still holding the stuffed goose, Bettina walked slowly into the living room. Far would be home from Skagen by the end of the week. Mor and Mormor would arrive soon, too. Bettina knew she had to have everything back to normal by then. But how?

She sat down on the same couch she had dozed on earlier that day, but now she wasn't at all sleepy. She gazed around the room. It was a comfortable living room. Mor's wooden rocker sat near Far's favorite stuffed chair. Photos of Bettina and Pia adorned the end tables. A smiling photo of Farfar, with eyes both reassuring and mischievous, seemed to be telling her something from a silver frame across the room. Floor-to-ceiling shelves of books arranged in no particular order covered one entire wall of the living room. It was an area of the house Mor often referred to as "the library," even though it wasn't actually a room itself.

Bettina rose to her feet and walked over to the library. Her eyes scanned the shelves, but she wasn't sure why. She knew the titles so well, she could list them with her eyes closed. There were picture books, and Bettina's stomach knotted as she read over Pia's favorite titles. There were carpentry books. And knitting and sewing books. There were volumes of history and folktales. There were cookbooks and books with maps of the world that so fascinated Bettina, she could spend hours engrossed in their pages.

But on this night, it was the long shelf of gardening books that caught Bettina's attention. She scanned over the titles. *Flowers Abundant, How to Grow Winter Vegetables,* and *You and Your Trumpet Vine.* At the end of the shelf, slightly crooked and sticking out just a little, was a large white book that Bettina barely remembered seeing before. But she had seen it. She had watched

Farfar pore over this very volume, his thick gray eyebrows tilted in deep thought. She gasped when she read the title: *How to Care for and Keep Your Nisse.*

Bettina took the book to the kitchen table. She pulled out a wooden chair and sat a moment before flipping open the cover. Heavily illustrated and written in great detail, the book was loaded with nisse sightings, nisse stories, and — most helpful — nisse facts.

Bettina turned to a chapter titled "The Nature of the Nisse" and read:

The nisse is at almost all times a kind creature. He takes great pride in belonging to a family, and he looks after the members of the family, both human and animal, with the utmost care and respect.

Bettina found these words comforting, knowing that if her little sister was at this very moment with a nisse, he might be kind and loving. She read on, hoping to find anything that would tell her why Pia might have been taken. Perhaps the book had a chapter on nisse who kidnap small children.

Bettina read more. She recalled long-forgotten facts that Farfar had once taught her — that nisse couples have only two children, always a set of twins; that nisse are keenly connected to nature, and that they sleep all day and frolic and play and work at night. She also learned many new things: Nisse are excellent woodsmen and navigators and cannot get lost, even in unfamiliar territory. And one cannot lie to nisse, as nisse can see right into the heart and know instantly if intentions are good or bad. And, according to the book, human-nisse encounters are rare, as the nisse will go to great lengths to remain unseen.

While she found all of this information interesting, it didn't tell her what she needed to know. At last she found a chapter in the back of the book, "The Disgruntled Nisse." She drew in her breath and began to read.

While most nisse are good-natured and can even be quite forgiving when overlooked by their families, every nisse has his limit. If a farmer and his family fail to appreciate their barn nisse, trouble can quickly begin.

*This is especially true on Christmas Eve, when every
nisse expects to be treated to rice pudding.*

"Oh no!" Bettina cried, remembering the Christmas
Eve telephone call and the disorder that followed. In all
of the holiday confusion, the Larsens had forgotten to
set out the rice pudding for their nisse!

She read on:

*Usually, a disgruntled nisse will retaliate with seem-
ingly random acts of mischief. Watch for orneriness
in the barn — items missing, flat tires on tractors,
animals in other animals' pens. Most of the time, an
unhappy nisse means no harm but only wishes to make
others aware of his displeasure for a short period of
time before things return to normal.*

Bettina thought of how she'd found the barn in utter
chaos and of the goats' feed.

*Of course, there is the occasional nisse who strays from
the ways of his kind and becomes not only disgruntled*

but dangerous. The nisse folk do not like to talk about this infrequent occurrence, and, therefore, the author of this book was unable to gather sufficient information except to say: Do not cross an angry nisse. It will not end well for you or your family.

Bettina shuddered. Had Pia fallen into the hands of a curious nisse? Or had she been taken by a more dangerous being?

She searched the book for any mention at all of a nisse taking off with a human baby but found nothing. She couldn't decide if that was a good thing or a bad one.

Bettina read into the night, forgetting that she hadn't eaten any supper. She continued reading into the wee hours of the morning until she was unable to focus on the blurry pages of the book. And finally, with her head on the kitchen table, the exhausted girl slept—which was good. She'd need to be rested for the day ahead. She'd need more than just sleep, though, if she was to find the nisse and bring baby Pia home.

Bettina woke with the first sliver of sunlight in the kitchen window, her neck stiff and her stomach growling. Anxious to set out in search of Pia, she quickly made a bowl of oats and milk and stirred in a few raisins. When she was finished eating, her stomach was satisfied and she felt calmer and more confident than she had the night before. Pia was not far, she was certain.

She put together a small lunch pack of rye bread, liver pâté, and sliced cucumbers. She wrapped it tightly in foil and added a few cookies, not knowing how long she might be gone. Along with a bottle of water and a small flashlight, she placed the food into a backpack and headed out into the snow. Bettina was surprised to see the winterfrost had remained overnight. She had never known winterfrost could last more than a day.

First she headed for the barn; the animals would need to be cared for before she could set out to search for Pia. She tried to sneak inside quietly, just in case the nisse was about. If she could surprise him, she might get a glimpse of him. Or better yet, she might catch him! She hadn't thought of what she would do if she actually caught a nisse. Perhaps she should have brought a box or some other container from the house. But the thought of a nisse trapped in a container of any sort sent a shudder right through her. Being trapped would surely make any nisse angry, wouldn't it?

Despite her stealth, Bettina found no one to surprise but the animals. It was, in fact, Bettina who was surprised when she stood before the feed bunks, brimming with fresh rations. Once again the barn chores were done. The animals were all fed.

She turned her head toward the hayloft.

"Thank you," she offered, hoping a sign of gratitude would please her helper. "Thank you."

Bettina pushed open the big barn door to look outside. She already knew that she'd find no tire tracks or footprints in the barnyard. Still, she scratched her head. Why would a disgruntled nisse go to such lengths to do her work for her?

There was no point standing around wondering. It was time for Bettina to find some answers.

Confession

Anyone who might have happened by the Larsens' garden on the December afternoon when Pia disappeared would have seen something so unlikely, so unbelievable, they'd have questioned their very sanity. It was a sight to behold, this little nisse carrying a baby more than twice his size. But, of course, no one did happen by the Larsens' garden on that December afternoon. And by the time Bettina Larsen woke from her nap to discover the baby missing, Klakke was deep into the forest.

Right about the time that Bettina was dashing about the garden in a panic, Klakke was making a discovery of his own. Despite the fact that he was many times stronger than a human, the child he carried was becoming heavy. The real burden Klakke bore, however, was not the physical weight of the child in his arms. It was the fact that he had no plan. The realization that he had probably made a mistake wore heavy on him like an oversize winter coat.

Baby Pia didn't seem at all alarmed. In fact, she seemed to rather enjoy the bouncy jaunt through the frosty forest. She giggled and reached for the soft white seedlings that sped by, knocking the winterfrost free from their branches and sending showers of frost to the ground below. Pia didn't seem to know or care where she was headed.

Klakke knew. There was only one place he could go, short of going back to the Larsens'. And there was no turning back, of that Klakke was certain. He'd already taken risks no nisse should take. He'd risked being seen, and for all he knew, someone could have been watching from that big kitchen window. Returning to the Larsens' home would just add to his ever-growing list of mistakes.

So onward he ran, toward the crooked oak, toward Gammel and the others. And toward certain judgment. What would Gammel say? And what would he do? What *could* he do, now that Klakke was in possession of a human child?

Klakke's tiny brown boots finally stopped at the base of the largest oak tree in the forest. There he gently laid the baby in a bed of frost-covered leaves.

"I won't be long, little one," he said, his voice high and a bit crackly with nerves. "Don't you be frightened, you hear me now?"

Baby Pia, seeing Klakke's small face, laughed. It was a hearty laugh from deep within her belly. She recognized the little man who just that morning she had caught a glimpse of, perched atop a bale of hay high up in the mow, while Bettina fed the animals. Once again Pia was filled with joy at the sight of Klakke.

Klakke, like most nisse, had a round face with rosy cheeks that looked like two small apples. His dark eyes sparkled, and his pointed red hat flopped just a bit to one side. At sixty-two years old, his beard was fully grown, and it was as brown as the curls that peeked out from beneath his hat. He would be at least a hundred before his beard and hair would turn gray.

Pia fussed a little when her new friend disappeared from sight. Her distress only added to Klakke's already-frazzled nerves.

"No, no. Don't fret. Klakke will be back," he said over his shoulder, and dove beneath a gnarled root at the base of the tree. Under the root, which stood only as high as the small nisse's hat, was a small oak door. He lifted the iron knocker gingerly and let it fall with a soft tap.

There was a long silence. At last, a plump nisse woman in a long moss-colored skirt and an embroidered white blouse opened the door. Her tall green nisse cap didn't droop like Klakke's. Long, tight braids tied with green ribbons hung on either side of her kind face. Everything about her was neat and tidy. When she saw her visitor, her eyes widened with surprise.

"Klakke, my dear!" she exclaimed, and threw her small arms around him. "You knocked so quietly, I didn't suspect it was you!" Klakke wasn't known to be the quietest nisse in the forest.

"Hello, Pernilla." Klakke shifted nervously, glancing over his shoulder to be sure baby Pia was safe.

The nisse woman took Klakke by the hand and pulled him inside. It had been a while since he'd been back to the house under the big oak. Klakke looked around and smiled. Nothing had changed. The wood-plank floor was neatly swept; the fire in the fireplace burned brightly, and Gammel sat before it, reading so intently he hadn't heard the knock on the door.

"Is everything all right, dear?" Pernilla inquired of Klakke, her voice low. "It's not quite dark, and you shouldn't be out, you know."

"Well, I, um," Klakke stammered, and avoided looking Pernilla in the eye. "I guess I ought to speak with Gammel."

Pernilla nodded, deep lines in her brow indicating her concern.

"Gammel, dear," Pernilla called. "Look who has come home."

Immediately she blushed, her rosy cheeks becoming even redder than before. Gammel would surely correct her, ever so gently. The old oak was not Klakke's home.

It never had been. Klakke's home was with the Larsens. But Pernilla was so fond of her younger cousin that she hoped he'd consider the house beneath the oak tree his second home.

Gammel, a stout old nisse with a long beard that flowed like a river of gray over his broad chest and abundant stomach, looked up from his book without getting up. He peered over the top of a small pair of round wire-rimmed eyeglasses.

"Well, I see," he declared, a wry smile curling up from both sides of his mouth. "Home he may be, but home he must go when he's finished."

At that, Gammel stood and strode slowly over to the young nisse. He, too, greeted Klakke with a hearty hug.

"Come," said the old gentleman. "Come sit by the fire and tell me what is new with the Family Larsen."

"Well, sir . . ." Klakke began, but he got no further. Two tiny nisse children burst in from an adjoining room.

"Klakke's here! Klakke's here!" they cried with glee, throwing themselves around his knees, dancing and cheering.

"Good day, Tika. Good day, Erik," Klakke greeted the little ones.

Behind them another gray-bearded nisse man, older than Klakke but not nearly the age of Gammel, entered the room.

"Good day, Hagen."

Hagen was a burly nisse, hardworking and strong. He greeted Klakke with a hearty hello and a handshake so firm, Klakke tried not to wince.

"It's good to see you, my boy." Hagen grinned and slapped the young nisse on the back.

"And you, too," Klakke agreed, but instead of taking a step farther into the room, he turned nervously to look at the door behind him. Gammel, being the eldest and wisest, picked up quickly on Klakke's behavior.

"Klakke?"

"Yes, sir."

"Have you someone with you?"

"Yes, sir."

"Well, then, who is it? Don't be rude and leave our guest standing outside in the cold."

Gammel took two quick strides toward the door, but Klakke stood in his way.

Gammel looked up in surprise.

"Klakke."

"Yes, sir."

"Look at me." Gammel's voice was stern.

Klakke obeyed and stared directly into the small black eyes of his elder. Gammel's eyes narrowed in thoughtfulness and then widened in disbelief.

"A human child? Klakke!"

"Yes, sir." Klakke broke eye contact with Gammel. He stared down at the neat wooden floor.

Pernilla and Hagen gasped in unison. Even the little ones became suddenly quiet. All eyes turned to Gammel, who didn't hesitate a moment.

"You must bring the baby inside," he declared. "Immediately."

Gone Again

Klakke wasted no time following Gammel's instructions. But when he emerged from beneath the big gnarled root, he was perplexed. There was no baby Pia. He was sure he'd left her right outside the house, at the base of the tree. Indeed, he could see the impression of her blankets in the frost-covered snow. He darted quickly around the oak, first in one direction, then in the other.

Klakke took off his cap and ran his plump fingers through his thick curls. Once more he studied the spot where he had left Pia. And once more all he saw was a small impression in the snow where the woven blanket containing the baby had been not long before.

Reluctantly, Klakke returned to the tiny house under the tree. This time he didn't knock. Instead, he gingerly opened the small wooden door and stepped inside. Hagen, Pernilla, and the children were waiting, excited to meet the human child, but Gammel stood by the fire, one boot on the hearth, stroking his beard.

Pernilla was the first to ask.

"Klakke, where is the babe?"

Gammel kept his eyes fixed on the fireplace.

"She . . . she wasn't there," Klakke stammered. "She's missing. I'm sorry, Gammel. I don't know what happened."

Nisse, by nature, are slow to anger, and Gammel had lived enough years to know that quick tempers lead to no good. He didn't scold Klakke. He didn't pace or appear to ponder the situation. But when Gammel finally looked up, his small black eyes had lost some of their sparkle.

"I feared something like this would happen."

He seemed to be speaking to Hagen, who nodded solemnly. Even Pernilla appeared to understand whatever it was Gammel wasn't saying aloud. Klakke looked from one nisse to the next, hoping to make sense of their unspoken words.

"Do you believe this is *his* doing?" Pernilla asked, eyes wide.

"I do," Gammel confirmed.

"'His' whose?" Klakke asked, his tiny toes tapping nervously on the smooth oak floor.

The older nisse ignored Klakke, talking as though he weren't there at all.

"But it's been years," Hagen protested. "What could he be thinking? Coming back now, after all this time?"

"Who's back? Who?" Klakke's body bounced involuntarily as he searched each nisse's face for clues.

"Perhaps he's returned to make amends." Gammel's voice sounded hopeful.

"Or to stir up more trouble," Hagen added, and suddenly Klakke knew who they were talking about. His hopefulness fizzled like fireworks on Midsummer's Eve.

Gammel seemed to already have a plan when he

finally addressed Klakke again. "We need the sister. You know what to do, Klakke," he said firmly.

Klakke nodded, determined not to mess up once more. He fled the house and ran deep into the forest, following the large tracks in the snow that could only have been made by Bettina's boots as she passed the old oak in search of her sister.

Chase

The forest was dim, but the snow cover brightened the ground beneath Bettina's boots. She had entered the woodland at the edge of the garden in exactly the spot where the winterfrost had been shaken loose from the seedlings. Before setting out, she had taken a long look across the field toward the Pedersens' house. A wispy string of smoke trailed up from the chimney, and she knew Rasmus and Lisa were home. Should she enlist their help? After a moment's hesitation, she turned again toward the forest and set out alone. If it was a nisse she was dealing with, she reasoned, the fewer humans involved, the better.

Bettina wasn't at all sure what she was looking for. The book had said that some nisse live in tiny underground houses beneath tree roots, so she kept her eyes low. She walked for almost an hour, through the most familiar parts of the forest. She walked through the sparse acres where Far and Mr. Pedersen had cut wood. She had been with them often, helping to carry logs to the truck parked by the roadside. But she didn't spend much time searching there, as few hiding places remained in a wood that had been cleared.

Entering the dense, untouched forest once more, she recognized some landmarks. There was the fantastically enormous spruce that she always believed would make the perfect Christmas tree for a family of giants. And then there was the crooked oak that every fall shed millions of fat acorns that Bettina would gather to entice the squirrels into the backyard in the winter. Far wasn't a big fan of squirrels in the garden any time of year, but Pia loved watching them from the big window. Only last week, Bettina had lifted her so she could babble and squeal at the squirrels as they tumbled over one another in the garden. Her sounds were so filled with joy and delight that even Far stopped what he was doing to come to the window and watch.

The vivid memory of Pia made Bettina move faster and deeper into the forest. The trees were close together now, pine and beech and oak and fir. With no path to follow, Bettina was well aware that she might be going in circles. But she had yet to come upon her own footprints. If she started to feel lost, she would retrace her tracks in the snow in order to return home.

It was another gray and cloudy day, an exact copy of the one before. The winterfrost clung to everything. The sun stayed away. After walking for what seemed to be half the day, Bettina started to become uneasy. She tipped her head to the treetops, where every now and then a sliver of cold December sky appeared. Was it noon? Later?

Even though Bettina was dressed for the weather, there was a dampness in the air that seeped through layers of fleece and crept with chilling fingers down her neck. How much longer could she continue searching before the cold drove her back home?

As she rounded a Douglas fir, a fat, snow-covered stump appeared, and she decided to sit and rest, using her forearm to clear the snow off the stump. She opened her backpack. She hadn't realized how hungry she was, and the rye bread and liver pâté tasted better than it ever did packed in a school lunch. She wiped her mouth and stared at the surrounding woodland.

Had she been here before? The stump told her that Far had been here and cut the tree that had once stood tall in this spot. Bettina squinted to see as far as her eyes would allow. The area didn't seem familiar at all. Everything was still. Nothing moved in the distance, and Bettina stood to zip her backpack, trying to decide whether to go deeper into the forest or to turn back toward home. Perhaps Pia had returned just as mysteriously as she had disappeared. But Bettina knew that was just wishful thinking. Her chances of finding Pia were better out here in the forest than they were at home in the living room.

Bettina's search continued. She'd trudged only a few feet when, out of the corner of one eye, she caught a glimpse of something moving. She snapped her head in the direction of the something. Whatever it was had stopped. Perhaps it was a rabbit. Or her own imagination.

She threw her pack over her shoulder and moved on. There it was again! This time she saw it for more than a second. It was small and lightning fast. And red. Red? What is red in the forest in wintertime? She darted toward the spot where she'd seen the flash of color and waited. Ahead, but not too far, she saw it again and she followed.

The small red blur continued to disappear only to reappear a short distance ahead, seeming to dare Bettina to keep up. She followed as closely as she could but never managed to get a good look at whatever it was that was leading her. Bettina soon found that keeping an eye on the ground and her surroundings at the same time was nearly impossible.

For half an hour, she hurried after the elusive blur. Every time she thought she'd lost it, a small glimmer of red would reappear. Eventually, Bettina became wary. Was this a trick? Did someone wish for her to become so disoriented in the forest that she would be lost for days?

Bettina stopped running. Nothing was familiar. She stared at the ground around her and saw a mingled mess of footprints, all of them her own. How could she have been so stupid? She had followed the little red blur blindly, and now? Now she imagined her parents coming home to find not one but both of their daughters missing!

Up ahead there was movement again. Bettina trailed it cautiously now, trying to find something familiar in her surroundings. She circled around a pine and found herself standing at the foot of the big crooked oak, the one with a million acorns near where Far and Mr. Pedersen had cut wood. How had she gotten back here when moments ago she was sure she was lost?

Bettina took one step toward the tree when her left boot got caught beneath a huge gnarled root. *Thwack.* She hit the hard white ground, arms out to her sides and facedown in the frosty snow. Still flat out on her stomach, Bettina used a mittened hand to wipe the cold snow from her eyes.

When she opened them, she quickly squeezed them shut again. It was a test; Bettina had to be sure her eyes were not playing tricks on her. She opened them slowly, drew in her breath, and forgot to let it out again.

It was no trick. Before her stood the tiniest man she'd ever seen. He had a round face with a mischievous expression framed in dark brown curls and a full brown beard. He wore a brown coat and boots. Red stockings covered his knees. And on top of his head was a tall red pointed cap that drooped just a bit at the point. The flash of red!

The little man gave Bettina a long, significant look, then darted under another root of the big crooked oak.

Discovery

Bettina blinked her eyes one more time as she lay flat on her stomach in the snow. It was a nisse! She was absolutely certain. He looked just like the little people in books, only more . . . real. But where had he disappeared to? All that lay before her was a twisted old tree root.

Pushing herself up on her elbows, Bettina used her teeth to remove one snow-soaked mitten. With her bare hand, she reached behind her and found the zipper on her backpack. She dug around until she had her hand on the small flashlight she'd packed. Clicking it on, she searched deep beneath the root. She half expected to find the little nisse man hiding there, cowering in the cold, perhaps as frightened of her as she was surprised by him.

Instead, what she saw made her draw in her breath yet again. The yellow glow of her flashlight illuminated a tiny wooden door, complete with a dull iron knocker, two wrought-iron hinges, and a latch. Should she . . . knock? As she contemplated how she would lift the minuscule knocker with fingers that seemed far too large, the door opened and an old, gray nisse man stepped out. He immediately shielded his eyes from the blinding light with one short arm. He was dressed similarly to the nisse Bettina had followed through the forest, only the point of his cap stood straight and tall.

And then the nisse spoke.

"Welcome, Bettina. We've been expecting you."

Bettina nearly dropped her flashlight. The older nisse man was talking to her! And he knew her name! She struggled to keep the light focused squarely on the tiny man.

"I . . . how do you know me?"

The man took a step to the left, still shielding his eyes with one arm.

"Would you be so kind as to lower your light just a bit?" he asked politely.

"Oh!" Bettina cried, feeling embarrassed. "Of course."

She aimed the light on the old man's boots instead, which cast the area behind the open door in shadows. Bettina was intensely curious, and she was sorely tempted to shine the light behind the man to see inside, if only for a moment. But the little man was being so nice, and he might have information that would lead her to Pia. She didn't want to offend him.

"You're looking for your baby sister," the nisse stated.

"Yes." Bettina breathed deeply. *His mention of Pia must mean he knows where she is!* "Yes, is she . . . is she in there?" It was a ridiculous question. The door itself was smaller than Pia.

The little man's round red cheeks grew redder. His dark eyes became a bit darker with concern. He shook his head, and his red cap swayed.

"No, my dear. I'm afraid she's not here. She should be. But she's not."

She should be? "What do you mean?"

The old gentleman opened his mouth to answer, then froze. "Shh. Listen," he said, his gray head and red cap tilted to one side.

Bettina listened. She heard nothing and was about to say so, but the nisse man was listening so intently, she tried again.

At first she heard only the sounds of the forest in the late afternoon. Sparrows making their final flights before settling in for the night. A squirrel's toes scratching across a fallen log as he hunted one last hiding place that might contain a nut for a bedtime snack. Just regular evening woodland sounds met Bettina's ears until . . .

"Bettina! Bettina Larsen!"

It was unmistakably the sound of Rasmus Pedersen's voice. And it appeared to be coming closer.

"You must not answer, Bettina," the old nisse told her.

"But it's Mr. Pedersen," she protested. "He's looking for me."

"If you want to find your baby sister, we must keep all other humans out of this," he told her with such authority in his voice that Bettina wanted to obey without question. But having had no previous experience with a real-life nisse, she was leery. She raised her flashlight just a bit. The odd little face that glowed in its beam looked honest and sincere.

"BET-TINA!"

This time Mr. Pedersen's voice was loud and clear and close by. Very close by.

Bettina looked once more at the nisse man. She could answer Mr. Pedersen. She could call out to him right now, and he would hear her. But something in the old gentleman's eyes convinced her to stay quiet. They were no doubt the kindest eyes she had seen since Farfar's.

"Come inside," the nisse said, pointing toward the tiny door.

"What? I can't . . ."

"Indeed, you can," he assured her. "Just reach for the door."

Reach for the door? Her hand alone was bigger than the door!

"BET-TINA! BET-TINA!"

Should she trust this small stranger more than a long-time neighbor?

"Now!"

Bettina, still lying on her stomach in the snow, glanced over her shoulder and saw Mr. Pedersen appear in the distance. When she looked back at the tree, the old nisse had disappeared and the tiny door was firmly closed.

She had only a moment to decide what to do next.

With her eyes closed tightly, Bettina thrust her hand into the space beneath the root. She felt the tiny latch and pushed down. The door opened, and with a sudden rush of air, she felt herself being pulled inside.

Small

Bettina stood eye to eye with three little people inside a cozy kitchen in a tidy house.

"Forgive me, Bettina," the old nisse man spoke, "for our rather rushed introduction. My name is Gammel. Welcome to our home."

Gammel extended his hand and Bettina shook it, amazed to see that *her* hand looked small in *his*!

"I did not have sufficient time to warn you," Gammel continued. "I know you must be a bit surprised."

Surprised, indeed. Bettina wasn't sure what she thought would happen when she reached for the small door beneath the crooked oak, but she never expected to find herself standing inside such a beautiful, brightly lit kitchen with a handful of . . . yes, she was quite certain they were . . . nisse.

Bettina may have been speechless, but her hosts were not.

"Hello, my dear. I'm Pernilla," said the nisse woman, her smile so broad and her eyes so kind, Bettina couldn't help but smile in return. "Gammel is my father."

Pernilla was neatly dressed in a crisp white blouse and a long green skirt that swished as she took a step toward Bettina and clasped her hand. On her head perched a tall cap just like the little nisse man wore, only Pernilla's was green. Long blond braids with just a hint of gray hung down either side of her face.

"Welcome," the third nisse chimed in — another man. His beard was also gray but not nearly as long as Gammel's. "They call me Hagen," he said, his voice deep but friendly.

Bettina glanced around. Where was the nisse she had chased through the woods? The frantic little man with dark curls and a droopy hat? He had seemed younger than Hagen — though age was a difficult trait to judge among nisse, she decided. Just how old was Gammel, the grayest of the nisse?

Even though she had a million questions swirling around in her head, Bettina couldn't for the life of her form one in her mouth.

"Come, everyone," said Pernilla. "Let's have cider."

Immediately, two nisse toddlers, one boy and one girl, appeared from behind Pernilla. They took Bettina by the hand and led her to a finely crafted oak table. *Twins,* she thought, *just as the book had said.* They each sucked on a pacifier, one pink and one green. The children remained at her side, gazing at her, pacifiers bobbing as they sucked.

"Meet Tika and Erik," Pernilla said as she busied herself at the stove, which was a grand piece of workmanship made of iron and painted green with an intricate heart-and-scroll design. "Please, dear," Pernilla said. "Sit."

Bettina sat at the beautifully carved table, her mind slowly registering what it was, exactly, that she was sitting on: an overturned walnut shell! She'd been too stunned to realize it earlier, but now it hit her like a fat acorn dropped from high above. If she was able to sit, feet dangling, on the top of a walnut shell, if she was able to look eye to eye with the old nisse she'd met outside, then something unbelievable — something *magical* — must have happened to her on her way in.

Gazing around the room in awe, Bettina noticed other familiar items being used quite imaginatively. In the corner near the fireplace, neat piles of dried leaves sat in an old bird's nest, ready to be used as kindling. Twigs were stacked for firewood. Fireflies perched in small glass globes filled the room with soft yellow light.

Gammel and Hagen joined Bettina. Pernilla carried four cups of steaming cider over to the table. Taking a seat, she whispered something to the nisse children, who detached themselves from Bettina's side and tottered to a rug made of thick green moss to play.

"Please, drink," Pernilla urged.

Staring into the caramel-colored cider in her cup, Bettina realized that the cup itself was a hazelnut shell. She drank, and the warm sweet-tart liquid on the back of her throat felt as good as it tasted.

She observed Tika and Erik as they took two large round acorns from a woven-grass basket and began to spin them on their pointy ends, like tops. Surely the acorns had been gathered from the ground beneath the big gnarled oak tree that Bettina had visited so many times. These were the same acorns that she had been able to carry by the handfuls, but here in the nisse realm, they were as big as softballs! Tika and Erik giggled as their spinning acorns slowed and then toppled sideways. Pia would love these young nisse and their toys! But Pia was nowhere to be seen.

Bettina didn't wish to be rude, but she hadn't come to socialize.

"You said Pia wasn't here," she began.

Gammel nodded in agreement. "I did."

"But you said she should be. Why?"

Pernilla sighed. Hagen cleared his throat and took a long drink from his nutshell cup.

Finally, Gammel spoke.

"Well, Klakke brought her to us earlier today. Do you know him?"

"Klakke?" Bettina had never heard the name before, but she suspected she'd seen this nisse man. "Is that who I followed here?"

"Yes, indeed. Klakke has been with your family for twelve years," Gammel explained.

"With my family? He lives with us?"

"In your barn. He cares for your family and your animals."

"Twelve years," Bettina repeated. "Why, he's been there since . . ."

"Since you were born," Gammel said, finishing her sentence. "He's done well for your family, that Klakke. We're quite proud of him."

"Oh," said Bettina. She had to ask. "And my family? Have we done well by Klakke?"

Gammel smiled. "Of course you have."

"But—" Bettina protested, remembering that just days before they hadn't remembered to be kind to their nisse. Their Klakke.

As if he knew exactly what she was going to say, Gammel held up a stubby finger to stop her.

"Klakke is young. He didn't take the time to learn the facts about your mormor's fall. If he had, he wouldn't have been so unhappy about the rice pudding."

"You mean the *lack* of rice pudding." Bettina sighed, wondering how Gammel knew about Mormor's broken hip.

Gammel nodded.

"Is that why he took Pia?" Bettina asked, as another sip of warm cider slid down her throat.

"No," Gammel answered slowly. "No, Klakke took your sister because he was curious. A bit foolish, too, I might add. But he did the right thing in the end. He brought her to me."

"But she's not here?" Bettina heard herself ask, confused.

"No, I'm sorry to say she is gone again. And this time, I'm afraid, it wasn't Klakke who took her away."

By now Bettina was having a hard time following the conversation. *Pia was here; Pia wasn't here?* Things weren't getting any better.

"Someone else took Pia? Who? Do you know?"

Gammel nodded.

"Yes, I believe I do. But don't you worry, dear girl. Old Gammel knows how to take care of this."

Bettina was about to ask Gammel whom he suspected took Pia when Hagen stood.

"Please excuse me," he said, finishing the last sip of cider from his cup, "but I must leave. There's much work to do outdoors now that night has set in."

Hagen removed his red cap and bowed his head to Bettina.

"It's an honor to have met you, Miss Larsen."

Then Hagen kissed Pernilla and was gone.

"I'm too old to go out and work." Gammel winked. "I do my best work by the fire these days."

"How old *are* you?" Bettina blurted, and immediately regretted how rude she sounded.

Gammel didn't bat an eye at the question of his age.

"Three hundred ninety-two."

Bettina's eyes grew round. *"Years?"*

Gammel's gray mustache turned upward with his grin.

"Years, indeed."

Was this possible? She tried to remember if the book

had said anything about the life span of nisse, but she drew a blank. Bettina turned to Pernilla, who nodded.

"Oh" was all she said. Could they hear the doubt in her voice?

"It is hard for you to believe," Gammel said knowingly. "It is old in nisse time, but it is ancient to the human way of thinking."

Tika and Erik, tired of spinning acorns, toddled over to the table. Bettina noticed the tiny pacifiers had nearly disappeared, dissolved like sugar. Were they *candy* pacifiers? Human babies would lose their teeth if they sucked on candy all day—and just think how long a nisse has to keep his teeth! But every nisse she'd met so far had a beautiful smile.

Pernilla had been following Bettina's gaze.

"We make them ourselves." Pernilla blushed. "From sugar beet syrup. We use the discarded beets left behind by the farmers in the fall."

Amazing! thought Bettina. The nisse world was so full of surprises, she was sure she wouldn't know about all of them even if she stayed a hundred years! But she had no intention of staying at all.

Bettina turned back to Gammel and the business of finding her sister.

"Hagen said it's dark now. I have to leave."

"Well, you're correct on one of two accounts." Gammel nodded. "It is dark outside now. Our day is just beginning, while yours is near its end. But there's no reason for you to leave. You must be exhausted."

"No," Bettina objected without thinking. "There are barn chores to be done at my home. And my sister — can you tell me where I can find her?"

"I'm afraid I don't know exactly. But I'll be working on finding out while you sleep."

Sleep? How could she possibly be tired? But the more she thought about it, the more she realized that she *was* tired. Her body ached from a day spent in the cold, damp forest, and her mind struggled to keep up with each event that was taking place.

Pernilla and Gammel shared a knowing smile and a nod. But it was Gammel who spoke.

"Besides," he told her, "your barn work is done for the night. I have sent Klakke to care for the animals for you."

Bettina heard Gammel, but his voice seemed to be coming from far away, and keeping her eyes open was becoming more and more of a challenge.

"But what about Pia?" Bettina asked, her words nearly swallowed by an enormous yawn.

Once more Gammel nodded.

"Hagen is making the necessary inquiries as we speak. We will work together to bring her home. I promise."

If Bettina had heard and fully understood these last words, she would have found them quite comforting. But she hadn't. Before Gammel finished talking, her head was on the table. She was fast asleep.

Breakfast Underground

Bettina woke the next morning in a cupboard. At least, that was the best way she could describe it.

Sitting up, she took in her strange surroundings. She was in a bed, and a rather comfortable one at that. She stretched as she tried to wake her mind and body simultaneously. She felt rested and calm for the first time since —

The previous day's events, including Pia's disappearance, rushed back to her, and if it hadn't been for this strange little closet she found herself in, she might have doubted whether any of it had actually happened. She closed her eyes and willed away the panic that threatened the peaceful feeling she'd had when she awoke. Gammel had promised to reunite her with Pia. That was what she thought she'd heard as she'd drifted off to sleep, and Gammel didn't seem like the type to make promises he couldn't keep.

Bettina turned her attention to her surroundings.

The little room was no bigger than the bed itself, which took up every square inch of the floor. There was a wooden ceiling and four wooden walls. Three of the walls were bare honey-colored oak, but the fourth wall appeared to be made of two doors with wooden handles. She was still wearing the same clothing she'd had on the day before, but someone had removed her boots and replaced them with the warmest, fluffiest white socks she'd ever seen.

Bettina reached out and opened one door slowly without even getting out of bed. Leaning forward, she peeked through the crack in the door. A familiar sense of disbelief washed over her as she observed the bustling kitchen of the nisse home.

Pernilla was busy at the green enamel stove while Hagen poked at the fire with what appeared to be a piece of fence wire. The little ones were dressed in nightgowns, and they played with yarn dolls on the floor beside matching wooden cradles with an intricately carved *T* and *E* on each end. They laughed and babbled unrecognizable words in sweet, soft voices.

Convinced once again that her memories of sipping cider in the kitchen of a nisse house just beneath the root of the giant oak tree were real, Bettina pushed the cupboard doors open all the way and swung her legs out of the bed and onto the kitchen floor.

"Ah, our guest awakes!" Pernilla smiled, wiping her hands on the apron she wore over a long white nightgown. Her long hair was unbraided, tied with a simple ribbon in the back. Her green cap had been replaced with a white one.

"How was your alcove? Did you get a good night's sleep in it?" Pernilla swished across the kitchen as she spoke.

Bettina thought sleeping in an alcove sounded much better than sleeping in a cupboard. Looking around, she realized that the entire wall was lined with doors exactly like the ones she had opened. There were sleeping alcoves for each of the nisse, and every door was beautifully carved with pictures of otters and chickadees and other woodland creatures.

"I slept very well, thank you," Bettina answered. "It was the finest bed I've ever slept in!" Pernilla's rosy cheeks grew a shade rosier.

"Come and eat some breakfast, dear. You'll need your strength for the day ahead of you."

The tiny home was so cozy, so magical, that if it hadn't been for Pia, Bettina wasn't sure if she'd ever want to leave. But finding her sister was her first priority. She only needed her coat and boots, and she'd be on her way.

On the floor just outside the alcove, she found her boots with her socks neatly folded and lying atop them.

"They were wet from a day of tromping about in the forest," Pernilla explained, yawning. "But I put them near the fire, and they're dry now."

"Thank you."

Bettina started to remove the thick, white socks she'd been wearing in the night, but Pernilla stopped her.

"You can keep those if you like. Klakke made them especially for you."

"He did?"

Bettina looked at the socks again and realized they had been knitted from the softest down of a thousand thistles. She marveled at how the prickliest plant could produce the most delicate fiber.

"He did. And he wants you to have them."

Bettina studied her tiny feet. Surely the socks wouldn't fit her once she was back to her regular size. She *would* she return to normal, wouldn't she?

"Come along." Pernilla motioned toward the table, where a fine spread of food awaited. "Help yourself," she prodded. "I must get the children ready for bed."

Suddenly it occurred to Bettina: She was the only one getting up. Everyone else was preparing to go to sleep for the day.

Everyone except Hagen, that was. He took a seat at the table.

"I can eat any time of day," he explained, patting the roundness beneath his belted coat. "You'll join me, won't you? It's never much fun to dine alone."

Although she was anxious to be on her way, Bettina smiled gratefully at Hagen and sat. He was obviously eating breakfast before bed for her benefit, and, besides, she had to admit she was hungry.

On her plate she found one fat fresh blueberry the size of a grapefruit. It could have been a meal in itself! *Where on earth had the nisse found such giant berries?* she wondered. But then she caught herself; it wasn't the berry that was big, but she who was small.

Beside the blueberry sat two hazelnuts and an enormous mushroom. Hagen's plate looked similar but with two mushrooms. Beside each plate was another smaller plate, brimming with fresh greens. How had the nisse folk found fresh leafy greens in the dead of winter? Surely they didn't frequent the supermarket in town!

"Lovely greens, aren't they?" Hagen said. "Few humans seem to realize what fabulous winter greens are hiding beneath the snow, even in December. There's chickweed, white nettle, cow parsley—even in the dead of winter. Of course, Gammel has quite a greenhouse set up beneath the next tree south, so we have a fresh supply of summer herbs all winter long. He grows dill and rosemary . . ."

Hagen rambled on about Gammel's greenhouse, but Bettina's thoughts were stuck on a single word. *Rosemary.* The herb in the goats' feed the day after Christmas! Had Klakke tainted the feed with Gammel's rosemary? She had a lot of questions for this young nisse who was supposed to be her family's guardian. And if she ever caught up with him, she would surely get some answers.

Bettina and Hagen each had an acorn cup of hot tea. She took a sip and recognized it as chamomile. Following Hagen's lead, she cut the blueberry in half with a silver knife, and she used both the knife and fork to cut up and eat the mushroom.

At last, the conversation turned to Pia. Hagen spoke between bites.

"We've spent most of the night discussing your situation," he told Bettina, his voice serious and thoughtful.

"And we've decided the best thing for you to do is to go home."

It wasn't what Bettina expected to hear.

"But how will I find Pia if I'm sitting at home?" she asked, putting down the fork and pushing her plate away. Suddenly she didn't feel so hungry.

"You must not look for her," Hagen said. "The situation is a family matter. Gammel knows just how to deal with it."

"But I have to do *something*!" Bettina cried. "Mor will be home in . . ."

What day was it? How long had she been in this little house under the tree? What once seemed very clear to Bettina now seemed lost in a blur of frost and leaves and roots and cider.

"Where is Gammel?" she demanded. And then, realizing she sounded quite cross, she softened her tone. "I'd like to speak to him, please."

Pernilla returned to the table, having settled the twins in their matching cradles. Their eyelids drooped, but their heads popped up occasionally as if they didn't want to miss anything the human girl said or did.

"Don't be upset, my dear. Gammel is doing everything in his power to find your sister," Pernilla said gently.

Bettina flushed with embarrassment. These kind folk had done nothing but try to help her since she stumbled upon them. She took a deep breath and continued her quest for answers.

"But," she addressed Hagen, "I thought Gammel said you were out making 'necessary inquiries' last night."

Hagen's eyes lowered. "I found out that what we suspected is true."

"And that is?"

"Complicated." Hagen wasn't providing the details Bettina had hoped for. She turned toward his wife.

Pernilla sighed. "You see, you and your sister — thanks to our dear, impulsive Klakke — have found yourselves in the midst of a . . ."

Pernilla fidgeted with her apron string. She was choosing her words cautiously.

". . . a dispute, let's say. A long-standing disagreement."

Hagen coughed. Or cleared his throat. Whatever it was, it was clearly intended to tell Pernilla she'd said enough.

"It's best to leave this to Gammel, dear."

Bettina had about a million questions, but something about Pernilla's voice and eyes, both assuring and kind, made Bettina feel at ease. She nodded. She would go home and wait. Gammel would sort everything out. The nisse seemed so sure of it. Then another thought occurred to her.

"How . . . how will I . . . ?" Bettina stammered, gesturing toward the door.

"You can leave the same way you arrived," Hagen answered with a smile.

"You should return to your normal size just as soon as you cross the threshold," Pernilla added, anticipating Bettina's next question.

They said their good-byes quickly. Hagen shook Bettina's hand and wished her luck. Pernilla hugged Bettina tight, and it felt for an instant like her own mother was holding her. She fought back a tear as she peered into the cradles where Tika and Erik had both given up and fallen asleep. When would Pia be home, sleeping safely in her own bed?

Sure enough, as soon as Bettina's hand pressed down on the door latch, she was pulled through the opening, standing once again in the snowy forest beside the big oak tree.

But much to her surprise, she wasn't back to her normal size.

And she wasn't alone.

Rounds

"Hello, Bettina."

It was Gammel who stood beside her in the heavily winterfrosted forest, a brown leather satchel in his left hand, and much to Bettina's dismay, there was no sign of baby Pia with him.

"Good morning, Gammel," she answered, hoping her disappointment wasn't too apparent. Fleetingly, she wondered if nisse call it morning when they are about to go to sleep.

"I trust you had a good night's sleep."

Bettina nodded.

"And Hagen has filled you in on the plan as it stands at this time?"

Again she nodded. "He said I should go home and wait. It seems no one is having any luck finding my sister."

"Oh, to the contrary, my dear," the old nisse replied, his round eyes twinkling. "A nisse without luck would be a terrible thing."

"Do you know something more?" Bettina asked breathlessly.

"I've learned that she's not terribly far. But I'm waiting to know more before we make our next move."

"How long do you think that will take?" Bettina asked.

"Patience, my dear. I know humans are accustomed to making everything happen at lightning speed, but you are now in our world, and here we take life at a little slower pace."

Gammel was right, she knew, but that didn't make all the waiting any easier to accept. And why was she still small? Pernilla had said she'd return to her old self once she'd crossed the threshold. Bettina was about to ask Gammel when he issued an invitation — one that surely would require her to remain nisse size.

"It's almost time for the nisse world to sleep. First, I must make my rounds. Will you join me?"

Bettina considered her options. Though she had not the faintest idea what Gammel meant by "rounds," she wondered if by accompanying Gammel, she'd visit more of the forest, perhaps places she wouldn't know to go to on her own. She could keep her eyes open for any signs of Pia. At this point, anything seemed better than Hagen's suggestion that she head home and wait, alone and helpless. Bettina agreed to accompany Gammel.

"Follow me," he said, his small legs setting off in a purposeful stride.

After walking only a short distance, Gammel stopped. Before them was a hole in the ground that would have seemed too small to notice under normal circumstances. But in her current state of tininess, Bettina thought it looked like a crater.

"Jump!" Gammel cried just as he leaped into the hole.

Was he crazy, this old nisse man? Crazy or not, he had disappeared down the hole. Bettina had no intention of following him blindly into the darkness below. That was, until two gigantic squirrels rounded the trunk of a nearby tree, one chasing the other in a downward spiral toward the ground—and headed right toward Bettina. As much as she tried to remind herself that they were not gigantic at all, and likely had no interest in her whatsoever, she couldn't stop her heart from pounding as they approached.

When the squirrels were so close that she could see their teeth, Bettina closed her eyes, held her nose, and leaped into the hole. (She had no idea why she held her nose—it just felt like something one should do when jumping in feetfirst.)

Down, down, down. Bettina landed with a *thud* at the bottom of a dark tunnel and immediately wondered if she'd made an enormous mistake. She couldn't see a thing! But within seconds, her eyes began to adjust to the darkness, and she was able to make out shapes before her. One, with his round belly and pointed cap, was unmistakably Gammel, but the other? She leaned in closely and found herself nose to pointed nose with a mole.

"Glad you joined us," Gammel spoke. "I was just checking on my friend here."

He turned to the soft-looking black mole, whose right front foot was wrapped in white cloth.

Gammel opened the leather satchel and dug around until he found a small tin.

"How's the digger?"

Bettina heard nothing, but Gammel responded as if he'd heard the mole answer.

"Ah, I see. Well, let's keep it wrapped another day or two. I brought your dinner."

From the small tin, Gammel produced a fat earthworm.

"I'll be back tomorrow," Gammel promised, and then, after a brief silence, added, "Thank you. I will certainly give your best to the family."

Back above ground, Gammel explained. "He cut it digging too near an old dump site. Probably on discarded glass or a tin can. He's in the excavation business.

Tunneling, you know. The moles are the first we call on when we start a new home underground."

Bettina could only nod, her voice snatched away by amazement and disbelief.

Their next stops brought more opportunities to help the nisse's forest friends. A trip to a mother rabbit's warren meant another leap into underground darkness, but this one ended in a much softer landing of rabbit fur. Gammel left piles of winter greens for the nursing mother, who was afraid to leave her brood to search for nourishment for herself. "First-timer," Gammel whispered to Bettina as they left. "She'll relax in a month or so, when she has her next litter."

At the entrance to a hollow tree, Gammel asked for Bettina's assistance emptying his bag of acorns, hazelnuts, and chestnuts. Bettina reached deep into the bag, passing each nut to Gammel, who stacked them neatly inside the tree until it could hold no more.

"Silly squirrels," he said, chuckling. "They hoard away nuts and such for the long winters only to forget where they've placed them. I like to help them out now and then."

Gammel closed his satchel and hoisted it back up onto one shoulder.

"Now where?" Bettina asked, fascinated by the journey. She'd lived next to this forest her entire life, but what she'd learned about its inhabitants in the past hour was far more than she'd ever imagined.

Gammel's frosty gray beard and mustache parted in a long, silent yawn. Of course. With every passing minute, more daylight seeped through the treetops, reminding Bettina that it was the end of a long day for Gammel. He was ready to return home and retire to his alcove.

"Home for both of us," Gammel replied. "Me to mine, you to yours."

The thought of returning to her empty house without Pia made Bettina's heart sink.

"What will I do there?"

"You will wait. You must trust me, Bettina Larsen. Do you trust me?"

Bettina nodded. She wanted to tell him that at this point she trusted him—and Pernilla and Hagen and even Klakke—more than just about anyone. But the knot in her throat told her not to trust her voice. She was certain if she tried to talk, she'd burst into tears.

Instead, she nodded. At least Gammel hadn't asked her to make any promises. She knew he believed she would go home and wait, but how could she? She'd go home, feed the animals, replenish her food supply, and then head out on her own to find Pia. As they parted ways, guilt tugged at Bettina's stomach, but even the guilt wouldn't keep her from looking for her sister.

Gammel watched the human girl wend her way through the woods toward home. By the time she was out of sight, she would be returned to her normal size once again.

It was true that Gammel hadn't asked Bettina to promise to stay home and wait. How could he? A nisse, after all, would never ask someone to make a promise he knew she'd never keep.

Remorse

Klakke had been on his best behavior since baby Pia had disappeared from beneath the big oak tree. He knew it was all his fault. He also knew that while he only took Pia out of impulsive curiosity, the one who took her from him likely did so for other reasons. His name was Ulf, and his character was known throughout the nisse world. That Pia was likely in Ulf's hands worried Klakke from the inside out.

Though young and often foolish, Klakke knew better than to try to intervene in baby Pia's rescue. The situation was for Gammel to solve, and Klakke would do best to just take care of the Larsens' farm. That was, after all, his responsibility and his alone. It was the reason he had come to Lolland in the first place. So, Klakke had returned to the Larsens' barn in the evening, just in time to feed the animals. The horses were unusually spookish, so Klakke sang every verse of "Jeg bœrer med Smil min Byrde"—"I Carry My Burden with a Smile"—as he went about his work. It seemed to calm Hans and Henrietta, and even the goats stopped their constant fussing to listen as well.

When Klakke fed the cats, the tiger mother dodged him twice, but she eventually came alongside and allowed Klakke to run his small hands across her back. When he got closer to her tail, though, she skirted sideways. Just in case.

But Klakke wasn't there to tease. He fed all the animals and carried fresh water buckets much larger than himself. With little effort at all, he hoisted the heavy buckets over his head. Keeping them steady was by far the harder task.

Klakke's guilt subsided one chore at a time. Working hard always made him feel better.

"There you be, my pets," he told the horses after he'd climbed the edge of the stall. He stood atop the wooden gate, looking eye to eye with Hans and Henrietta. The horses were used to his presence, and they continued to noisily chomp their grain while he spoke.

"Seems I've upset the way of living here at the Larsen place," he admitted. "But don't you worry, my friends. 'Cause Old Gammel's going to fix everything right back to the way it was. And he's going to do it real quick. Before the mister and missus come home."

Hans and Henrietta bobbed their heads as if to communicate their understanding. It was enough to satisfy Klakke. He hopped nimbly from the stall wall to the barn floor below.

By the time he finished all the barn chores, the sun was ready to creep up over the barren sugar beet fields. And when it did, Klakke knew he'd best be out of sight. On a normal day, he would have climbed the ladder to the hayloft and slept the day away in hidden comfort. But this was not a normal day, and Klakke was feeling an added responsibility to the Larsens. Especially to young Bettina.

Klakke slipped through the barn door, opened just a crack, and hurried to the wood room. There he restarted the fire that had gone out; Bettina shouldn't come home to a cold house. It would be bad enough, he thought, that she must come back to a house that was empty and quiet. With a fire roaring inside the stove, Klakke was sure the house would be warm before Bettina returned. He was sure Gammel wouldn't have sent her anywhere else but home. Morning light had not yet broken the horizon, so Klakke sneaked into the kitchen and flipped on a light over the sink. He smiled as the soft yellow glow washed over the room.

Back in the barn, Klakke settled himself into the warm golden straw in the loft. He was tired, and sleep came quickly. But it didn't last long.

Klakke awoke to the sound of Felix's deep barking. *Vo-vo-vo.* Then a moment of silence. Then *vo-vo-vo-vo-vo-vo.* Someone must be outside.

Klakke ran to the front of the hayloft and pushed open the window the tiniest bit. Felix was darting in circles around the barnyard, his tail wagging furiously. Klakke's gaze turned toward the road and saw unmistakably that the neighbors were making their way toward the Larsens' house. He drew in his breath and closed the door. He was sure Bettina would be home by now. There was nothing he could do to help. Bettina must handle this one on her own.

Visitors

Bettina expected the house would be cold and dark, but when she emerged from the forest at daybreak, she noticed three things: a small light glowed from the kitchen window, smoke curled from the wood-room chimney, and everything around her was normal size again. Gradually, during her walk back from making rounds with Gammel, she had grown tall again.

No longer being tiny came as a relief. It was the first two observations that worried her. With a light on and the fire going, it sure looked like someone was home.

Surely Mor or Far couldn't have returned so soon. Or could they have? Had her sense of time been altered while she was nisse size? She took off running toward the door.

Inside the wood room, she saw that the fire had been stoked recently. The firebox was full, and warmth filled the adjacent kitchen. Bettina removed her winter coat and snow-covered boots, remembering how tiny they had been when she was nisse size. To her amazement, the white thistledown socks had grown right along with her, and they remained warm and snug on her feet. But despite that bit of evidence, Bettina's recollection of the night in the house under the tree was becoming fuzzy, more like a dream than reality.

"Hello?" Bettina called as she stepped inside the house. She turned off the light above the sink. There was enough daylight now, even though it was turning out to be another cold, cloudy winterfrost morning just like the one before. This string of identical days only added to her inability to keep track of what day it was.

"Anyone home?" she asked, her heart pounding.

Then just to be cautious, she added, "I'm back from my walk in the woods!"

There was no response, and Bettina knew she was alone. The clock on the kitchen wall read 7:47, but she ran to look at the one on the fireplace in the living room. When the second clock confirmed the time, Bettina sighed. She found comfort in knowing that she was back to a place where time was measured and meant something. She put a kettle of water on the stove for tea and then sat down at the kitchen table to gather her thoughts and make a plan.

Outside, Felix let out a loud bark. Then another. She dashed to the window above the kitchen sink and moved the curtain aside. Oh no!

Rasmus and Lisa Pedersen were walking down the road toward the Larsens' house.

Bettina scrambled from the kitchen. She took the stairs two at a time and quickly changed into clean clothes. At the bottom of the steps, she tossed the clothes she'd been wearing into the laundry room just as she heard the familiar *ting-a-ling* of the bell inside the wood-room door.

Mr. and Mrs. Pedersen were standing in the wood room when Bettina opened the kitchen door. Their smiling faces covered up a long night of worry.

"Good morning, Bettina!" Mrs. Pedersen greeted Bettina with a hug.

"Hi!" Bettina returned brightly. She stood in the doorway, not offering to let the Pedersens in. Mor would be aghast at her rudeness had she been there to witness it, but Bettina could hardly risk their poking around and asking after Pia.

"Lisa and I are just checking in on you girls," Mr. Pedersen told her. "Wanted to be sure all is well with your folks away."

"Oh, thank you so much. Yes, we are fine. We're doing great!" Bettina tried to sound convincing.

"I'm glad to hear that." Mr. Pedersen sighed. "We, uh, we were here yesterday. And we couldn't find anyone."

Bettina took a deep breath. She didn't like to lie, but she saw no other way out.

"Yesterday? Oh, we went sledding all day! You know,

this winterfrost is so beautiful, we simply had to be out in it," she explained.

"Oh, I agree with that! I spent a good deal of time outdoors myself yesterday. Walked through the forest, and it was breathtaking out there," Mr. Pedersen said.

He didn't mention that he'd called her name just before she entered Gammel's house. Bettina sighed with relief. Perhaps that would be her last lie.

Mrs. Pedersen was a petite woman, younger than Mor, with no children of her own yet. But she adored baby Pia. Mrs. Pedersen tried to see past Bettina.

"Where is the baby?" she asked.

"Pia?" Bettina tried not to stammer. "Pia's sleeping right now."

Mrs. Pedersen frowned. "Still sleeping? It's nearly eight o'clock. Are you sure she's all right, Bettina?"

"Oh, no," Bettina explained. "I mean yes, she's all right. But no, she's not *still* sleeping. She's napping. Again. That little girl was up at five in the morning, all bright-eyed and ready to play. So, we got up very early, had our breakfast, fed the animals, and she's back to napping now. She's sleeping cozy in her—"

Bettina stopped midsentence. She knew the pram where Pia usually napped was right behind her in the kitchen, next to the patio doors where she'd left it after she'd discovered it empty.

". . . bed," Bettina finished quickly.

"Oh, that's too bad." Lisa Pedersen sighed. "I was hoping to hold her awhile. Is she walking yet?"

"Almost." Bettina smiled, ever the proud sister. "I planned to teach her to walk before Mormor gets here, but . . ."

Now it was Bettina's turn to sigh. *But I can't teach her to walk if I don't know where she is,* she thought.

". . . but she has a mind of her own, I'll tell you," she said instead. "She'll walk when she's good and ready!"

The Pedersens laughed along with Bettina at Pia's stubborn streak.

Then there was a moment of awkward silence. A long moment in which Bettina wasn't sure what to say next and the Pedersens seemed reluctant to end their brief visit.

Suddenly the teakettle hissed. It started out low but quickly grew to a piercing wail. Bettina let out a long breath.

"There's my water for tea," she stated matter-of-factly. Both Bettina and her neighbors were well aware that Mor would have invited them in for tea.

Again, uncomfortable silence. Except for the teakettle, whose call was becoming more urgent with each passing second.

"Well, then, we'd best be on our way," Mr. Pedersen said. "You tend to the kettle — though do be careful."

"Yes, dear, please be careful. And if you need anything at all, you know where we are," Mrs. Pedersen added, still talking even as she walked backward out of the wood room and into the barnyard. "Anything."

Bettina assured her neighbors that she would call if necessary, closed the door, and took the screaming kettle from the stove. She realized that she probably should have said something about the kettle waking Pia, but she hadn't thought of that. She wondered if the Pedersens had.

She made a cup of tea and honey, and from the

kitchen window she watched Mr. and Mrs. Pedersen making their way back to their farm. She took a small sip of tea. It was too hot to drink.

As much as she'd wanted the Pedersens gone, Bettina wished them back again. The silent kitchen, the entire house, felt empty. Empty like the pram that stood there before her, a painful reminder of all that had gone wrong in such a short time. Gammel had promised to find Pia, but what if he failed? Bettina tried to imagine what would happen if Pia wasn't home when Mor and Far returned. She closed her eyes and imagined Mor's stricken face and Far's disappointment. Tears burned beneath her still-closed eyelids.

Bettina opened her eyes and looked out over the back-yard. The winterfrost remained, still and silent. Not a single frosty blade of brown grass moved. The sea must be as still as glass, Bettina thought, remembering summer days when her family had followed the fjord to the sea to soak up the breezes and lie on warm sand.

The Larsens would visit the sea again, she vowed. Pia would toddle in the sand and splash in the cool water with Bettina while Mor, Far, and maybe even Mormor watched from their blankets in the sun.

Outside something caused Bettina's thoughts to return from the sea. But what? She scanned the garden, but everything was still. She turned from the window when it caught her eye again—an unmistakable flash of red.

Action

Just minutes earlier, Klakke paced the haymow floor and went up and down the ladder a dozen times. What were the Pedersens saying to Bettina? Or—perhaps worse—what was *she* saying to *them*? Finally, when Felix started barking once more, Klakke peeked out the window in the loft. Rasmus and Lisa Pedersen were leaving! They were all waves and smiles as they headed away from the house, but their smiles didn't last long. They appeared to be deep in discussion as they walked down the driveway toward the road.

It seemed Bettina had averted disaster. Klakke was proud. The more he knew of Bettina Larsen, the more he liked the girl. She reminded him somewhat of his twin sister, Klara. Confident. Dependable. And not afraid of adventure. He'd only seen Klara a couple of times each year since he'd left Falster, and he missed her wonderful giggle.

Klakke was sure he wouldn't be able to go back to sleep now. In fact, he wasn't sure he *should* go back to sleep. The Pedersens' visit had made him realize the urgency of Bettina's situation. How could Gammel expect them to just sit while he tried to work things out? Wouldn't it be better to have *two* nisse looking for Pia? Besides, Klakke had created this mess. He should be the one to resolve it. That is what any mature, reliable nisse would do. Klakke was convinced that he must take action, and the sooner, the better.

Leaving his post was a serious matter, and one that Klakke didn't take lightly. He knew he could be entering dangerous territory, so he thought it best to leave a note. If the worst happened and he never returned, perhaps Gammel or Hagen would come by and at least they'd know his fate.

"I've gone to Ulf's abode to retrieve the stolen child. If danger befalls me, please take care of the Family Larsen and their animals," he scribbled on a small piece of paper, which he placed high in the mow where only nisse eyes would think to look.

Klakke knew he should take the path that led directly from the back of the barn to the edge of the forest. It was daylight, and taking the shortest route to cover made the most sense. But he couldn't help himself. He took instead the garden path that led behind the house. It was the same way he had gone the day he took baby Pia from her carriage. It was because of the big kitchen window that he took this path today.

Klakke moved quickly through the Larsens' back garden. When he reached the woods, he turned and stood very still. Sure enough, she was there. Bettina stood with a cup of tea in front of the big window, and he was certain she saw him. Then, right before he darted into the forest, Klakke gave Bettina a smile and a tip of his pointed red cap. Just to let her know that everything would turn out fine.

Swept Away

Klakke wasted no time as he headed through the forest. He was breaking the rules yet again, being outside in broad daylight. But a small voice inside his head told him that he had but one chance to undo the wrong he had done—and that chance was now. He knew that there were those who believed him too young to handle the responsibility of a farm. And he knew of one nisse in particular who had been waiting twelve years for Klakke to slip up. Now he simply had to bring baby Pia back home.

As Klakke hurried along, he thought about what he had done back at the Larsens' patio. It is rare that a nisse makes his presence so obvious to a human, especially in human territory. Perhaps this is why most humans don't believe in nisse—they find it impossible to believe in that which they haven't seen with their own two eyes. But Farfar Larsen knew without a doubt that the family shared their farms, fields, and forests with nisse. Klakke had heard Farfar speak to him in the barn, even though he was careful to stay hidden away in the mow.

Klakke continued onward, his mind racing as fast as his tiny booted feet. Bettina was so much like her grandfather. Willing to look for the unseen. Klakke wished there were more folks like Bettina and her farfar in the world.

Klakke ducked beneath a small log and over a mouse's nest on the other side. He waved to the startled mouse mother and continued on. Ahead was a large clearing where tall dead grasses blew in the winter breeze. Klakke had never crossed the clearing during the daytime. He glanced around to make sure he was alone—that the pesky Pedersens hadn't decided to take a stroll through the woods — and then set off.

Klakke was clipping along at an impressive speed, his boots *pat-pat-patting* rhythmically over the grassy ground, when he noticed his right foot missed the earth below. He looked down. His left foot also missed the grass by an inch or more. Then his right foot. Then his left. With every stride, his feet were getting farther and farther from the ground beneath him!

Nervously, Klakke turned to look over his shoulder. He saw gray and white feathers and a long, sharp beak holding tightly to his brown coat.

"Gammel!" he cried as the clearing below became a tiny patch of land among the forest. Soon even the trees — including the giant oak — grew tiny.

"GAM-MEL!" the little nisse called again, but to no avail. He was high above the forest now, being taken far, far from his home in the beak of a seagull.

Witness

Bettina tripped through the snow-covered forest. She'd been following Klakke for nearly half an hour, not at all sure where he was headed, but praying that if she followed him, she might find more clues that would help her find Pia.

Bettina had hurriedly layered clothing and stuffed her feet into her boots, and moments after spotting Klakke near the forest's edge, she'd slid out the back door and rushed after him. Thoughts of Gammel brought less guilt now that she had an excuse to be out in the forest instead of sitting at home. She told herself, *I'm look-ing for Klakke, not Pia.* But there was no denying it: Bettina knew that looking for Klakke also meant looking for Pia.

Continuing through the forest in the direction she had seen Klakke go, she stepped over a small hollow log and noticed a nest of mice burrowed on the other side. Just a few days ago, she probably would have passed over the nest without even seeing it. Doing rounds with Gammel had made her more aware of what was happen-ing in the forest around her.

When she reached a clearing of dried brown winter grass, Bettina stopped and sighed. In this tall grass, she would never be able to see little Klakke, if he was even out here at all. What now? Feeling defeated and a bit foolish for following Klakke in the first place, Bettina turned for home.

Then she heard something odd. *"Ammmmm-ullllll!"*

It came again, small and faint, and growing more dis-tant with each second.

Bettina turned her eyes to the sky above. Gray winter clouds hid the sun, and a lone bird flew overhead. *Just a bird,* she thought. A bird that appeared to have caught a mouse in his beak. Bettina squinted. When did mice start wearing red hats?

"Klakke!" she cried. But before his name was even out of her mouth, the bird and its prey had disappeared over the trees. Klakke was gone.

Sent

Bettina hadn't dreamed she'd be back at the gnarled oak tree so soon, but there she stood, not at all sure how to get the attention of the nisse inside. Should she reach her hand under the root and knock? Or just open the door?

With thoughts of Klakke hanging helplessly from the beak of a seagull, Bettina got down on her belly and reached for the handle. She closed her eyes, held her breath, and pushed down. A familiar pull tugged at her hand, her arm, then *whoosh!* Bettina found herself standing in the kitchen of the tiny house under the oak. She was indeed small again.

Bettina had expected the whole nisse family to be standing before her, but the kitchen was empty and the house was silent. A faint glow from a small red ember in the fireplace cast the only light in the room. There was no sign of the fireflies; their glass globes sat empty. It appeared that no one was home. Bettina's heart sank. What would she do now? She'd lost her sister and Klakke, too. She was counting on Gammel to know how to help.

In the corner near the fireplace, something stirred. Bettina took a cautious step closer and saw an enormous gray mouse asleep on a bed of moss on the hearth. The mouse rolled over and stretched. His scratchy toes reached as far as they could, his mouth opened in a great sleepy yawn, and then his whole body relaxed before he opened one eye. When the large rodent caught sight of Bettina, he leaped from his bed.

Bettina jumped back. Normally she wasn't afraid of mice, but given her new size, this field mouse was intimidating. Much to her relief, the animal made no move in her direction. Instead, he opened his mouth and squealed. Loudly.

"*Squeeeee, squeeeee!*"

And again. "*Squeeeee!*"

Bettina stared. What should she do? Was he talking to her? Yelling at her? In the tiny kitchen of the nisse house, the mouse's squeak echoed like a fire alarm. And Bettina soon realized that an alarm was exactly what the little mouse intended to be.

Cupboard doors opened in all directions. Bewildered nisse stepped from their sleeping quarters. *Alcoves,* Bettina remembered Pernilla had called them. Of course, Bettina had arrived in the middle of the nisse night.

First out was Hagen, followed by a yawning Pernilla from the same alcove. From another door, Gammel emerged with a look of grave concern. When he saw Bettina standing before him, he turned to the mouse by the hearth and placed a finger to his lips.

"Shh," he said calmly, and the gray mouse immediately ceased his squealing. "Thank you, Erling. You've done a good thing."

Quite pleased with himself, the rodent gave Bettina a satisfied nod. He circled the mossy green mat once, twice, and then settled comfortably back in place and closed his eyes. Bettina was amazed.

Finally, Gammel spoke.

"Bettina, my dear, something serious has happened."

It wasn't the first time Bettina had found it hard to determine if Gammel was asking a question or conveying a fact. But then she remembered that the old nisse had a way of seeming to know things even before they were told to him.

"Yes, I saw Klakke just now, and—"

Bettina hesitated. How could she tell them that their beloved Klakke was gone? They all looked at her so patiently while she fumbled for the right words.

". . . and he . . . he has been carried away by a large bird!"

There was silence as the nisse shared glances with one another that Bettina found difficult to interpret. Finally, Pernilla began to laugh.

"Again?" she sputtered.

Hearty laughter burst from deep within Hagen's

round belly. Even Gammel chuckled and stroked his long, gray beard.

"It's the third time this week," he explained.

Bettina sighed. "So Klakke's OK? He's not in any danger?"

"Oh, no, my dear," Pernilla assured her.

From their cradles in the corner, two small heads lifted to see what was going on. How the twins had slept through all the commotion made by the mouse alarm, Bettina would never know!

"I'm sorry," Bettina apologized. She was beginning to wish she'd never come. "I woke the entire household and for nothing."

"Don't be silly, sweetheart," Pernilla said. Then she turned to her husband. "Hagen, would you please tend to the little ones? Perhaps a pacifier would quiet them. Take lemon for Erik, and Tika adores mint. I'll put on some water for a bit of ginger-root tea."

Hagen turned his attention to the twins while Gammel relit the fire. Erling, the watch mouse, snored softly in the corner.

"Sit with me, Bettina," Gammel instructed.

They sat in two chairs made of willow twigs, bent to form perfect seats and rockers, and tied together with foxtail stems. Bettina found her chair quite comfortable.

"Tell me more," Gammel said, "about where you saw the hawk lift Klakke into the air."

"It was just over in the grassy clearing not far from here," Bettina explained. "Except it wasn't a hawk. It was a seagull."

Gammel's thick gray eyebrows furrowed. Bettina had seen that look of concern before.

"A seagull, you say?"

"Yes," said Bettina. "Is that bad?"

"Well . . ." Gammel stroked his beard and tapped one stubby index finger against the side of his round face. "This changes things a bit."

"They were already high in the sky when I saw them, but I'm sure it was Klakke. It sounded like he was calling your name, perhaps."

"Hmm" was all the thoughtful old nisse said for a long while. And then, "Which way did they fly?"

"North," Bettina answered without hesitation. Years

of walking the woods with Far had instilled in her an excellent sense of direction.

That one word seemed to be all Gammel needed to make up his mind.

"You're going on a journey, my dear."

Bettina was startled. "Me?"

"Yes, and it is a journey you must take alone."

It wasn't what she'd expected to hear. "Am I looking for Klakke?"

"I believe you will find Klakke," the old nisse told her with such confidence that she believed it, too.

"And Pia? Will I find Pia?"

"Where Klakke has gone, Pia has also gone."

Bettina stared into the fire, which had come back to life. Its chaotic flames danced with no rhythm or direction. Like the thoughts in her head. Wasn't it crazy for Gammel to send her off on a wild-goose chase? But what were her choices, really? She had to find Pia. And Gammel was counting on her to find Klakke, too.

"Pernilla will prepare a small pack for your journey. And then you must be on your way," Gammel told her.

"But, first, there are some things you must understand, Bettina. We nisse are a peaceable and private lot. A woodland nisse, such as myself, is at one with the trees and animals of the forest. Barn nisse, such as Klakke, care for the livestock and the family who live nearby. There can even be an occasional house nisse, living in the home of a human, but most of us are a bit too private to share our living space with humans."

Bettina marveled at Gammel's last remark. He had allowed *her* into *his* living space, and she felt honored.

"The nisse's relationship with others is rarely complicated. We respect and care deeply for all living things," Gammel continued. "With that said, I will admit that occasionally a rift occurs between two or more of our members. One nisse in particular, a nisse who once lived close by, had a falling out with the rest of us a few years ago. So serious were his actions and the resulting consequences that he left Lolland. His name is Ulf."

An uninvited chill seemed to have entered the room. Even the fire's warmth couldn't hold back the shudder Bettina felt grab her shoulders. She remembered what

she'd read about wayward nisse; could Ulf be dangerous? She was so wrapped up in listening to Gammel's
story, she nearly forgot she had a part in it.

"And now," Gammel concluded rather abruptly,
"you must find Ulf."

The little kitchen under the enormous oak was
so quiet, Bettina could hear the watch mouse softly
snoring.

"But why me?"

"You are a Larsen, are you not?"

"Yes, but—"

"Ulf's mistakes affected the Larsen family more than
anyone else. Heaven knows, I have tried for many years
to set things right with Ulf. Just yesterday I sent Hagen
to speak on our behalf, but Ulf sent him away. But not
before Hagen saw evidence of your Pia. She's there with
Ulf, Bettina, just as I had suspected. And only you can
set things right again. Perhaps Ulf will return your sister
to you if he knows he has the forgiveness of the family
he disappointed."

"Won't you come with me?" she nearly whispered.

"I'm sorry to say that due to past circumstances, my presence would not help your situation," Gammel answered.

There was a sadness in his voice that tugged at Bettina's heart and filled her head with even more questions. A small knot began to form in Bettina's throat. She felt as if she'd swallowed a hazelnut whole. *What did Ulf do to the Larsens? When?* Bettina thought it best to ask the most important question first.

"Is Pia — is she safe?"

Gammel peered over the top of his glasses. "I cannot lie to you, Bettina. I do not know Ulf's motives, and his behavior has been unpredictable in the past."

Bettina's heart sank. But Gammel continued. "I do believe, however, that Ulf's grudge is with those of us in the nisse world. He was always quite fond of the Larsen family."

A slow sigh of relief slipped from Bettina's lips. It wasn't much, but she'd take what little hope was offered. Now for the more practical questions.

"Where will I find this Ulf? How . . . how will I get there? And what am I supposed to do once I find him?"

"Everything will become clear to you in due time."

Despite her apprehension, despite her worries, something about Gammel's demeanor calmed her and gave her confidence. He believed in her, and that seemed to be enough to get her started. The next thing she knew, they were on their feet and Pernilla was hugging her.

"Turn," Pernilla instructed. Bettina obeyed and Pernilla placed a small backpack on her back.

Gammel took Bettina by the hand and led her to the door.

"But my size . . . How will I . . . ?" she started to ask, but Gammel interrupted her.

"Your size will always work to your advantage," he assured her. Then he placed her hand on the door handle, and she was whooshed from the comfortable kitchen to the frosty forest beneath the giant gnarled oak.

Bettina stood a moment and stared at the forest that surrounded her. It was familiar, yet different somehow. The giant oak seemed to have somehow grown even taller. And the leaves under her feet were as large as dinner plates. It wasn't until Bettina spotted an acorn the size of a boulder that she realized it had happened again!

Instantly, she turned to reach for the door, but she couldn't find the root.

"Gammel!" she called. "Gammel, I thought I would be big! How will I ever get out of the woods if I'm the size of a sapling?"

Bettina circled the oak twice looking for the root that hid the small door, but she could not find it. This would never work.

Your size will always work to your advantage.

They were the last words Gammel had spoken to her. Being tiny out here in the big world didn't feel like an advantage at all, but Bettina trusted Gammel.

She found a small rock and climbed on top of it to get a better look around. There must be a reason for her smallness. But how on earth would she get to Ulf? Walk? It could take days. Or weeks. And she didn't even know where to go.

A sharp snap in the frosty undergrowth of the forest to her right startled her. Behind a tree, a large white goose like the ones in the Pedersens' barnyard appeared.

Normally, Bettina didn't mind geese, except for the Pedersens' gander, which at certain times of the year became very protective of the geese and was prone to charge at anyone who came too close. This was no gander, but Bettina still felt wary. She could easily be flattened by one of those webbed feet.

The white goose meandered through the trees. As she moved closer, Bettina recognized the old goose. She *was* one of the Pedersens'. Bettina was sure the mother goose was lost, as she'd never seen a farm goose so far from a barnyard. Wild geese, yes. The Pedersens' geese? Never.

"Shoo!" Bettina shouted, surprised at the big sound coming from her small mouth. At least her voice hadn't shrunk with the rest of her. "Go home!"

She had hoped that her loud command would startle the wayward goose back in the direction of the Pedersens', but she only came closer. Could she even see Bettina, given how small Bettina was?

"HONK!" The goose's enormous golden beak barked directly at Bettina. No doubt. She could see her just fine.

Bettina slid from her rock perch and scampered quickly around the back of the giant oak. On the other side, she held her breath and waited. *Out of sight, out of mind,* she thought.

"HONK!"

Bettina's heart nearly stopped. One of the goose's enormously round black eyes was staring her in the face.

"HONK!"

"Stop that!" Bettina scolded, momentarily forgetting that the animal was at least nine times her size.

The Pedersens' goose continued to honk at Bettina. And Bettina continued to tell the goose to go home. But the goose didn't budge. She came closer and closer, honking incessantly but not angrily. It was as if there was something she wanted Bettina to know. Or do.

"What do you want?" Bettina threw her hands in the air. "I don't have time for games. I'm supposed to go somewhere, and I haven't got a clue where or even how I'm going to get there!"

Her outburst stopped the goose's squawking. Very quietly, very deliberately, the white goose stepped right up to the tiny girl. She bent her long, sleek neck down and placed her head on the ground at Bettina's feet. And she waited.

"What are you doing now?"

Bettina was exasperated. But the Pedersens' mother goose had also run out of patience. With her large round beak she snatched Bettina's backpack, taking Bettina right along with it.

"What . . . HELP!" Bettina screamed.

How would she ever find Pia and Klakke if the old white goose ate her for lunch?

But instead of swallowing her, the goose stretched her long neck around and gently placed Bettina on her back. And then she took off running!

Still a bit dazed, Bettina threw her arms around the goose's neck and squeezed.

Sensing her passenger was now holding on tight, the mother goose stretched her long white wings and leaped forward. With strong, steady beats, the goose pushed higher and higher until they were soaring far above the forest, high above the barren sugar beet fields, and heading north.

North toward Klakke. North toward Pia.

Crossing

Lolland's winter landscape became a blur beneath Bettina as she and the Pedersens' goose soared into the clouds. At first, Bettina held on to the goose's neck with a grip so tight, she feared the goose might stop breathing midflight. But as the bird's powerful wings settled into a steady rhythm of up, down, up, down, Bettina's heart stopped racing and her own breathing fell into perfect time with the flapping. Only then did she loosen her grip and relax.

The white goose seemed to know exactly where she was going. When Bettina gathered enough courage to look over one side, she saw houses and barns that looked like toys, and fields and farms that were laid out in squares as if someone had thrown a patchwork quilt of whites and grays over all of Lolland. She tried to look for landmarks that would tell her where she was, but quickly discovered that looking down while flying didn't agree with her stomach. She drew in a long, deep breath and kept her eyes on the clouds ahead.

Time stood still. Had she been flying an hour? A day? Or only a few minutes? She risked another quick peek down. No more winterfrost. They had left behind a winter wonderland and entered a dismal gray landscape. The sun, just as in the days before, was nowhere to be seen.

Timelessness offered Bettina plenty of opportunity to think. What would this angry nisse Ulf be like? Bettina imagined she might have to bargain for Pia's return, but what did she have to bargain with? She came with only the backpack Pernilla had provided. Back at home, the Larsens had very little that others didn't have. There were some of the latest electronic gadgets, computers, and such, but Bettina had a hard time imagining that these would be of much use to a nisse.

The Larsens owned a few antiques, passed down from Farfar's family. One treasured heirloom was a shiny gold pocket watch that had belonged to Farfar's grandfather. Perhaps a nisse was like a leprechaun, taking interest in objects of value, like gold. But the book hadn't mentioned such a trait, and having met Gammel, Pernilla, and Hagen and having been in their home, Bettina was doubtful that gold would appeal to any nisse. Even a wayward nisse.

Up ahead, the empty beet and hay fields and forests became fewer, and small clusters of buildings appeared. Bettina took a deep breath and looked straight down. Below her, she spied a church steeple and a grain elevator. They were flying over a town. Buildings were packed tightly along curving streets that led right up to what looked like water. Bettina sat up straight and strained to see past the goose's neck. Sure enough, on the horizon Bettina spotted boats. Lots of boats of all sizes as well as ships crawling into the harbor. Bettina knew where they were. But the goose showed no signs of descending. They wouldn't be landing in this familiar coastal town. Bettina and the goose were flying directly for the sea.

Many hours seemed to pass with nothing but steel-gray clouds above and a matching sea below. Bettina's eyes grew heavy, but she was afraid to sleep for fear she'd loosen her hold on the goose's neck and tumble from the sky. Far down in the sea, she could see the Askø ferry, and she had a hunch they were following it to the small island north of Lolland. It made sense that anyone trying to avoid people would hide out on Askø, especially in the wintertime. In the summer, the island was popular with tourists packed into summerhouses. But in the winter, Askø was nearly deserted.

Sure enough, just as the Askø shoreline came into view, the Pedersens' goose started her slow and steady descent toward land.

Askø

It was high noon when the Pedersens' goose set down lightly on the icy island of Askø, but the sun was nowhere to be seen. There was no winterfrost here. No magical winter wonderland. Just steel gray and cold. By the time Bettina slid from the goose's slick white back, freezing rain had begun to fall and the wind drove every drop angrily toward her face. They had flown over the ferry dock, over the dock house, and over the lonely summerhouses that occupied the shore. They had flown into the heart of the small island, where Bettina could not see one sign of humanity whatsoever. A perfect place for an unhappy nisse to live. But where, exactly?

"Well?" Bettina turned to her feathery tour guide. "What now?"

The goose honked once and took three running steps. Should she run after the goose? Perhaps she was showing Bettina which way to go next. But before Bettina had time to decide, the Pedersens' goose flapped her wings several times and took off toward Lolland.

"Wait!" Bettina yelled into the wind. "Don't leave!"

But the big white goose never glanced back.

"Thanks for the ride," Bettina muttered.

She was getting used to her new state of tininess, but even so, she found the enormity of everything around her quite overwhelming. She'd been left in a field of dried brown winter grasses that swayed around her and towered overhead like flagpoles. It was impossible to see over their willowy tops, so she started walking in the direction of the small forest she'd seen before the Pedersens' goose had landed. A nisse trying to hide would likely make a home in the forest, wouldn't he?

At her current size, even small rocks created an

enormous challenge. And even though the island wasn't very big, Bettina knew that her little legs would only carry her so far before the gray sky overhead turned to black and darkness set in. Would she even make it to the woods by then?

Above, Bettina heard a sharp cry. *Ah-ahh! Ah-ahh!* A seagull soared over, then dipped low. Bettina ducked, protecting her head with both arms. She'd seen how a gull had snatched Klakke. Was she next?

But the gull sailed back into the gray clouds overhead, and his cries faded as he disappeared over the sea. Bettina lowered her hands, her heart pounding. She continued toward the woods, still aware of the occasional forlorn call of a distant gull. Soon there were no more cries, and an eerie silence filled her ears. Cold, icy rain fell. The air hung around Bettina's neck and shoulders like a wet towel, and she shivered. Askø in winter was not the lush, sunny haven she and her family had enjoyed on summer holiday.

With only the squish of her boots in the wet earth below, Bettina pressed on. At last, she came to a place where trees and bushes began to replace the tall grass.

As she walked, the trees grew taller and closer together until she found herself deep in a wooded area. Overhead, the breaks between the treetops seemed few and far between. At least she was out of the rain, if not the cold.

Now what? Bettina wondered. There were no paths, no way to tell in which direction an unhappy nisse might have made his home. She looked for anything that might be slightly out of place. A thin layer of ice covered the leafy forest floor. Brown dried leaves clung precariously to half-bare winter bushes. Nothing stirred. Not even a leaf moved in the cold, still air.

And then Bettina heard something. Not a seagull. Not a bird of any sort. A whimper? Her heart raced once more. Pia?

Bettina stood perfectly still and listened, her eyes scanning the dull, lifeless forest for some sign of movement. Again, a sound. A tiny call.

"Bettina?"

Bettina sighed. It wasn't Pia.

She searched the underbrush to no avail.

"Bettina. Up here."

She lifted her eyes from the forest floor to the tree-tops. A small figure, red hat tilted to one side, hung awkwardly by the back of his coat on the lowest branch of a birch tree. His brown-booted feet dangled, swinging impatiently.

"Klakke!"

With an embarrassed grin, he waved one small hand. "Hi, Bettina."

Bettina grinned back. Despite his role in Pia's disappearance, she had developed a certain affection for Klakke, and that fondness now warmed her chilled bones from the inside out. She wanted to throw her small arms around the little fellow and squeeze him with delight, but she couldn't. He was well outside of her reach, even on the lowest branch.

Klakke's cheeks grew pink, perhaps from the cold or more likely the awkward situation in which he found himself.

"I seem to be stuck." Klakke sighed. "I think that crazy bird meant to drop me at Ulf's house, but instead I got caught in this branch."

Klakke was indeed in a predicament. And Bettina

wasn't at all sure how to get him out of it. She reached as high as her small arms would allow. She missed him by what seemed to her to be several feet, but in reality was probably only a few inches.

"Don't worry, Klakke," she said. "I'll get you down."

Bettina searched the forest floor for something that might be useful, but everything seemed either too small to be of any use or too large for her to pick up on her own.

"There!" Klakke pointed to a very long stick.

Under normal circumstances, it would have been a small thing for Bettina to pick up the stick, but at present, her circumstances were far from normal. The stick was enormous and as big around as a log!

"Just try it!" Klakke's legs swung higher with excitement. "You may be surprised."

Bettina shrugged and bent to grab the stick. To her amazement, it was incredibly light for something so large.

She dragged it close to the tree.

"How . . . ?"

"Nisse strength," Klakke explained.

"But I'm not a nisse."

"No, I guess not, but somehow you managed to become our size, and it looks like you've got the strength to go with it."

Your size will always work to your advantage.

Bettina smiled. Gammel was right again.

"I, um, don't want to seem impatient," Klakke began, "but could you . . . ?"

"Oh! I'm sorry, Klakke!"

Bettina rested one end of the long stick against the branch where Klakke hung. The other end she planted firmly in the wet soil.

"That looks sturdy enough. Can you climb down?"

Klakke grabbed the stick. He pushed and pulled and turned and twisted, but he still couldn't loosen the back of his jacket collar from the tree.

"You'll have to come up," Klakke said apologetically, his face redder than before.

Bettina stared up the slanted stick. It seemed a long way from the ground to her new friend. She hoisted herself onto the makeshift ramp, and, much to her surprise, she was able to scramble to the top just as quickly as she had climbed the ladder to the haymow in the barn at home many times before. By the time she reached Klakke, Bettina was beaming with confidence.

"Don't you worry," she told him. "I'll have you unhooked in no time!"

It only took one try for Bettina to unsnag Klakke's brown coat from the tree.

"*Whee!*" Klakke hollered as he slid down the stick to the ground below. "I'm free!" (Klakke wasn't used to spending too much time in any one spot.)

Bettina laughed and descended with a bit more caution.

"Thank you, Bettina Larsen!" Klakke stared at her intently, and a huge grin spread across his round face.

Bettina was excited to meet Klakke face-to-face at last. This was the nisse who lived in the barn, watching her do her chores, sometimes helping. And sometimes, perhaps, causing a little mischief? She remembered the time just days before when Pia had giggled while peering high into the barn's rafters.

"It's very nice to meet you," Bettina said. She extended her hand, which Klakke shook enthusiastically.

"You were very brave just now, climbing up to save me," he told her. "You remind me of someone."

"Do I?" Bettina was curious. "Human or nisse?"

"Nisse, of course," Klakke answered. He knew so few humans. "She's my twin sister, Klara."

"You have a twin?" Bettina started. "Ah, yes, of course you do! I should like to meet her someday."

Klakke looked wistful for a moment. "I should like to see her again someday," he said. "It's been far too long."

The young nisse said no more about his sister. He just continued to smile at Bettina, perhaps a bit tongue-tied in her presence. It was, after all, his first nisse-human interaction, except, of course, for the brief moments he had spent with the adorable baby Pia.

Pia. The very reason both Bettina and Klakke had come to Askø. And although neither could be certain, both held on to the same hope. The hope that Pia was close by. And the hope they'd see her again very soon.

Facts

As if he could read her thoughts, Klakke said to Bettina, "We should go speak to Ulf."

Bettina was surprised.

"You know where to find his home?"

"It's not far." Klakke motioned to a narrow path barely visible at the base of the very same tree that had snagged him.

Together, they set out. When their tiny boots fell into step with one another, Klakke began to speak.

"Gammel sent you, I suppose," he said.

"Well, yes. He said Hagen was certain that Pia was with the nisse named Ulf. And that Ulf would need my forgiveness for something he'd done to my family years ago. But, Klakke, I don't know what to do when I find him!"

The young nisse shook his head. "Oh, what a fine mess I've created!"

The pair walked over crisp, frozen leaves, barely making a sound in the winter afternoon.

"I think I can help you, Bettina. There are some things you should know. For starters, Ulf once lived on Lolland, but he left years ago."

Bettina nodded. Gammel had told her as much.

"Did you know Ulf?" Bettina asked. "Were you friends?"

Klakke smiled, but the smile didn't last long.

"Yes, I knew him. But, no, we weren't exactly friends."

"Oh."

"We were — we are — cousins."

"Oh!" Bettina was surprised.

"Ulf is older than me. He had a farm and a family to

care for on Lolland. And he took his work quite seriously," Klakke told her.

"So, Ulf wasn't a woodland nisse but a barn nisse."

"That's correct. But then something happened. The worst that could happen to a barn nisse."

Bettina pondered Klakke's words. What was the worst that could happen to someone charged with caring for a barn filled with animals? Her eyes grew wide.

"Oh no! He did something to harm someone's farm animals?"

"Well, yes, in a manner of speaking. His negligence led to an animal's death. A very special animal. It was the farmer's favorite horse."

Bettina felt immediately sorry for the innocent horse and farmer. She adored horses. It was a passion passed down through generations of Larsens. Far was quite proud of Hans and Henrietta. And Farfar? Oh, Farfar had treasured every one of his horses. Most especially a beautiful white Arabian gelding named Kasper. Farfar had spoken of Kasper with such admiration and sadness, as Kasper had met an awful fate when someone left his stall unlatched one night . . .

The heart inside Bettina's chest stopped beating for just a moment.

"Klakke, when? When was Ulf a barn nisse? And whose, Klakke? Whose nisse was he?"

Klakke sighed.

"Now you see why I must tell you this before you meet Ulf. Before I came to Lolland, he was your nisse. Well, not yours, exactly, as you were just a newborn when he left."

Bettina's pace slowed. Ulf was the Larsens' nisse.

"Tell me more, Klakke. Tell me everything."

"Well, Ulf cared for your family for nearly a hundred years. He knew your far when he was just a boy. And your farfar, too. He took care of the animals, slept in the very mow I sleep in now, watched out for the family. He was very conscientious."

"How, then, did he forget to latch the horse's stall?"

"That question is the very source of this conflict, Bettina."

"I'm afraid I don't understand, Klakke."

Klakke sighed. "Ulf maintains it was an accident. His father suspected otherwise."

"Ulf's father?"

"Ulf's father, Gammel."

Oh! Things were starting to come together. Ulf was Gammel's son, Pernilla's brother.

"And all this happened . . ." Bettina began.

". . . twelve years ago," Klakke finished.

"When I was born?"

"When you were born."

Bettina had more questions, but Klakke had stopped walking.

"There it is." He pointed to the tree before them.

"Where?" Bettina stared but saw nothing that looked like a nisse home. No dark doors beneath craggy roots. No small openings between the bark.

"I don't see —" she began.

But then something caught her eye. A line. A very straight line among the curved lines of leaves and twigs. She narrowed her eyes and moved closer, and as she did, she gasped.

There, at the base of the tree, was a small brown nisse-size house. Its earthy colors blended perfectly with the surrounding woodland. Its roof sported a thin layer of frost. Upon closer inspection, Bettina realized that the roof was shingled neatly with row after row of perfectly laid pinecone scales. Ulf was as resourceful as every other nisse she'd met.

"This is it?" she asked Klakke.

Klakke nodded.

The tidy little bungalow seemed too neat and well kept to be the home of Ulf. Wasn't he supposed to be disgruntled, unsociable? This place looked most hospitable. Maybe it was a trick. Like the witch's candy cottage that lured Hansel and Gretel too close.

"Should we . . . should we knock?" Bettina asked.

"You do it," Klakke urged. Of course, he wasn't necessarily anxious to see Ulf. And Ulf couldn't possibly be happy to see his younger cousin, who had taken over his duties with the Larsens.

Bettina hesitated no longer. The time had come. Klakke held his breath as she lifted the iron knocker and let it drop. From inside came a muffled reply.

"Come in."

Bettina opened the door, and the two stepped inside.

The kitchen was surprisingly similar in design to

Gammel's. An empty fireplace, an elaborately detailed enamel stove, and a line of closed alcoves along one wall. But the place was darker and emptier. It lacked the warm, homey feeling that the nisse family had created in the house under the oak back on Lolland.

Bettina scanned the room for Pia but saw no sign of a baby. Or anyone else for that matter.

"Hello?" she called. "Is anyone here?"

"Back here," came the same low voice.

Bettina and Klakke shared a look of apprehension before Klakke nudged her toward a long, narrow hall. Slowly they crept down the hallway until it opened into a large gray room, where a grapevine rocking chair sat before yet another fireplace. This fireplace was aglow with a roaring fire, but even that didn't seem to bring much warmth to the room. A pair of brown-booted feet rested against the edge of the hearth and kept the creaking rocker in motion.

"That is Ulf," Klakke whispered, pointing to the dark figure whose back was turned.

Then he ducked behind Bettina and hid.

Ulf

The boots on the hearth abruptly stopped the rocker, and the mysterious Ulf stood to face his guests. Bettina could feel every muscle in her small body tense up. Behind her, she felt Klakke tremble.

Ulf was a bit taller than either Gammel or Hagen, and a good bit taller than Klakke. He was dressed in traditional nisse garb, minus a hat. Short gray hair, a bit disheveled, topped his head, and a short gray beard fell just below his chin. He was thinner than any of the nisse men, perhaps a sign that he lacked the good cooking of a kind nisse woman.

But it was his eyes that most set him apart from the others. They were small and round and blacker than the darkest of Danish nights. Bettina held his gaze for only a moment before looking quickly away. His eyes were as cold and empty as the room in which they stood.

"Bettina Larsen," Ulf said flatly. "I knew you would come."

"I didn't have much choice," Bettina answered hotly, then feared that she might anger the nisse with her temper.

His face showed no emotion. "You were sent."

Once again, Bettina was faced with trying to discern a statement from a question. He seemed to know that Gammel had sent her.

"Yes, I was. I am here to find my baby sister," she stated, trying to sound as if she had some control over the situation.

Ulf nodded. "In good time."

Then he tipped his head to one side.

"I can see you back there, Klakke," he said. "You're not fooling anyone."

Klakke slowly stepped out from behind Bettina.

"You can? Oh. Sorry," he said shyly. "And, um, hello."

"What are you doing here?" Ulf asked sharply.

Klakke stayed near Bettina for support.

"I . . . I had to find the . . . the baby," Klakke stammered.

"Well, it seems you've succeeded."

Ulf took a step to the side. Bettina gasped. There, behind the rocker, stood a wooden cradle much like Tika's and Erik's. In it, baby Pia slept soundly.

Bettina rushed to peer inside the cradle. Pia looked peaceful and content in the cozy cradle. She was swaddled in a thistledown blanket, as soft as the socks Bettina still wore.

"Pia!" Bettina whispered, mesmerized by her sister's sweet face. She gently stroked the baby's plump cheek, being ever so careful not to wake her. "I was afraid I'd never see you again!"

"Your sister is fine," Ulf assured Bettina. "I have let no harm come to her."

Bettina turned toward Ulf. "Why?" she asked. "Why did you take her from Klakke? What could you possibly want with a human baby out here? In this empty, lonely wilderness?"

Tears burned Bettina's eyes as her anger pushed its way to the surface. It occurred to her that she may have just answered her own question. Had Ulf taken Pia for company? This dark and lonely cottage might only be made brighter with the laughter of a child, especially one as darling as Pia.

"We shall talk," Ulf said.

Still leery, Bettina peeked once more at the peaceful Pia. Although she desperately wished to scoop up her sister and smother her with kisses, Bettina knew it was best not to disturb the sleeping baby until everything was resolved with Ulf and she could take her home for good.

Ulf motioned for Bettina to take the rocker, which she did. He planted himself on a hand-carved wooden stool. Klakke, strangely still and unusually silent, sat on the hearth close to Pia but far from Ulf.

There was a long pause. Bettina gazed at Ulf, who seemed uncertain how or even where to begin the necessary conversation.

Finally, he spoke.

"Not long ago—longer to your way of thinking than to mine—I lived happily on Lolland."

"You knew my family."

Ulf nodded. "Quite well. Not only knew the Larsens but cared for them. For two generations."

Despite her best efforts, Bettina simply could not picture Ulf as a young, happy nisse, smiling, whistling, and going about his business on the farm. "And so you knew Farfar?"

At the mention of Farfar, Ulf's face softened just a bit.

"Indeed. From the time he was a boy, your grandfather spoke to me, though he never once saw me. Every day, without fail, he came into the barn and greeted me. But then, many children acknowledge their nisse; it's the adults who pretend we don't exist. But your farfar was different, Bettina. Long after he abandoned his childish ways, after he grew to be a stout and sturdy man, he still talked to me daily."

Ulf's words came as no surprise to Bettina. Farfar

had been absolutely certain about the existence of nisse in the forest and on the farm. And even when Bettina's mother would cluck her disapproval over Farfar's tales, Farfar would stand firm in his belief.

"Farfar believed in nisse," she told Ulf. "He told me so many times."

"Of course he did. Even though I never let myself be seen. That's what made your farfar special, Bettina. He believed without seeing."

"Farfar's gone," Bettina told Ulf. "Did you know?"

Ulf's stoic face turned suddenly sad. It was a look just like the one Bettina had seen in her own mirror many times: Ulf also missed her grandfather.

"I did know. My sister sends word of important happenings on Lolland." Ulf sighed. "I miss him, but I guess I've been missing him and the rest of the Larsen family for twelve years."

Ulf glared at Klakke, who'd been uncharacteristically subdued.

"It wasn't my fault they called me," Klakke said, defending himself.

Ulf grumbled. "No, but they did, didn't they? They called you to do the work I'd done, and done well, for many years. A young nisse like you!"

Klakke wasn't going to take this sitting down. He stood up, tall and straight, and Bettina thought he looked altogether different from when he'd hid behind her just a short time before.

"It was your own carelessness that got you into trouble!" he snapped.

Horrified, Bettina glanced toward Ulf. How would the already-disgruntled nisse react to such an outburst from his younger cousin?

But much to her surprise, Ulf looked resigned. "It's true," he confessed. "I've never denied that I was to blame. But I still maintain that the punishment didn't fit the crime."

As much as she didn't really want to take sides, Bettina had to admit that it seemed Ulf had been judged rather harshly for something that was an accident.

"I don't understand why Gammel sent you away."

"Oh, he didn't send me anywhere," Ulf said. "I left

on my own. Out of anger. My father didn't believe that what happened to Kasper was an accident."

"But of course it was! You wouldn't have let anything happen to Farfar's horse on purpose. Right?" Bettina held her breath until Ulf answered.

"Of course not!"

Bettina let herself breathe again.

"Why, then, would your father believe you would? This is your chance, Ulf. Tell me your side of the story."

Ulf shifted on his stool.

"All right, then. Twelve years ago, all was well at the Larsens'. I was doing my job just as I had done for a hundred years before. And the greetings from your farfar, Bettina, were the highlight of my day. Then one spring day, the younger Mr. Larsen and his wife brought home a new baby."

"Me?" Bettina wondered aloud.

"Yes, Bettina," Ulf continued. "It was you. I was overjoyed. I had been around when your far arrived and even when your farfar came into this world. There's no greater joy than when the family welcomes home a new babe. And your arrival was no exception.

"Your grandfather was so proud. So very proud, in fact, that he didn't linger in the barn that day. So eager was he to see his precious granddaughter that he forgot to speak to me! For a week after you came, there was not a single greeting, not a word of acknowledgment from your farfar. I was shaken. Afraid it had finally happened."

"Afraid what had finally happened?" Bettina asked.

"It struck me, Bettina, that your farfar had become like all other grown-ups. He had concluded at long last that his nisse friends were not real."

"Oh no! That's not true! He never stopped believing, Ulf."

"I know that now," Ulf said, his voice heavy with regret. "But I didn't then. Your farfar's abandonment — or what I believed to be his abandonment — hit me harder than I expected. I was so preoccupied with my self-pity one afternoon that I didn't check Kasper's stall latch. I should have. I had checked and double-checked all the locks and latches every night for as long as I'd been a barn nisse. But that day I didn't. Burdened with my dark thoughts, I climbed up into the mow and went to sleep. And by morning, it was too late."

"He had gotten into the feed room," Bettina finished. Oh, if she'd heard Kasper's story once, she'd heard it a thousand times. Farfar had always blamed himself for not latching Kasper's stall that night. It was a cautionary tale, told over and over again on the Larsen farm. A horse left before feed will eat without stopping. The sweet grain will be too much to resist, and he'll colic and die before he gets his fill.

Ulf looked down. He was silent.

"But that wasn't your fault, Ulf." Bettina tried to console him. "Farfar was careless, too! He was distracted and eager to return to my side. The blame isn't all yours!"

Ulf looked up, his eyes filled with pain and regret.

"It is the job of the barn nisse to take care of the animals, especially when the humans can't do it themselves. Your farfar is not to blame, Bettina. It was my oversight that caused Kasper's death, my distraction — not his."

Bettina knew it was useless to argue the point further.

Clearly Ulf believed that he alone was responsible for the death of Farfar's prized horse. But one thing still confused her.

"Even if it was your fault," she began tentatively, emphasizing the *if*, "why did you leave? Surely anyone who knew the circumstances would have forgiven you."

Ulf frowned and Klakke appeared agitated. Clearly Bettina had hit a sore spot.

"Anyone but my father. He had heard me complaining about your farfar's lack of attention. He knew that I was angry, and my anger dismayed him. He was afraid I'd left the stall unlatched as a way of getting back at your grandfather." Ulf flushed. "I hadn't, of course, but it didn't really matter; I had done what no barn nisse should ever do, and that is to allow harm to come to one of the barn animals."

"And this punishment you spoke of?" Bettina asked.

"I was removed from my post." Ulf scowled.

Klakke remained calm this time. "Gammel called me," he explained. "He called me from Falster to take Ulf's job."

Bettina looked from young Klakke to his older

cousin. Oh, how humiliating it must have been for Ulf to be replaced by the younger, less-experienced Klakke!

"I don't think Gammel meant it to be for long," Klakke went on. "I think he only meant for it to be a short while. For you to think about what had happened."

Ulf made a sort of snuffling sound. "As if I could think of anything else! Besides, I couldn't stay and watch *you* care for the Larsens," he told Klakke. "And my father knew that."

"And so you left," Bettina said, understanding at last. "You left Lolland and came here to live your life alone."

Suddenly it occurred to Bettina that Ulf hadn't stayed away completely.

"But you came back," Bettina said. "You were at Gammel's just recently. You took Pia!"

Ulf nodded. "I did come back. But it wasn't to cause further mischief."

Klakke made a noise that sounded very much like a snort. Ulf paid no attention.

"Pernilla sent word that now might be a good time to come. Gammel, she said, was softening in his old age. And, to be honest, it is his age that worries me most. He's three hundred ninety-two. He won't be here forever."

Bettina hadn't thought of the nisse losing loved ones to old age the way she'd lost Farfar.

Ulf took a deep breath. "I came back to Lolland because I wanted to make amends. But, thanks to Klakke, nothing went as planned."

Spoken Truths

Klakke leaped from the hearth.

"Me? What did I do? You're the one who took Pia from me!"

Ulf threw another log on the fire. He didn't seem to be in any rush to share his side of the story. At last, he answered.

"Sit back down, Klakke, and I'll tell you."

Klakke sat.

"It was the day after Christmas. The twelfth Christmas I'd spent alone here on Askø. That's a lot of years for humans. A lifetime, for you, Bettina."

Bettina nodded.

"Though it's but an eyeblink in the nisse world, it felt like a lifetime to me as well. And I made up my mind that it was time. Time for me to return to my family. Time to look into my father's eyes and let him see my regret and sorrow.

"When I arrived on Lolland, the winterfrost was breathtaking. I wandered through the forest, enjoying its beauty. I remembered how much your farfar loved the winterfrost, Bettina, how he'd become especially talkative to his nisse on those days—for who can experience a winterfrost without feeling that magic is all around them? Inspired by these memories, I decided to check on the Larsens. I was anxious to see how young Bettina had grown while I'd been away and if she took after her grandfather in any way.

"I got to the Larsen farm, and all was quiet. Too quiet. Though it was early, I saw no smoke from the chimney. I saw that the car was gone, and I wondered if the family was gone for the holidays.

"I crept inside and listened. I could detect the sounds of movement from one of the bedrooms above, but not the other. Pernilla had told me that the family had a second child—another sweet daughter. Were the girls home alone? No wonder the fire had gone out! I went into the wood room and stoked it back to life."

"*You* stoked the fire?" Bettina asked, remembering how she'd awakened to a warm house.

Ulf nodded.

"Thank you," said Bettina.

A hint of a smile appeared on Ulf's face. "It felt good to be of service to the Larsens again. But I knew my next stop was to look in on Klakke in the barn. Why had my cousin let the fire die out overnight?"

"You were checking up on me?" Klakke asked, bristling.

"I knew that something must be off for you to have neglected the fire. And when I entered the barn, I could see that the animals needed tending, too. But you were hiding out in the haymow, sulking."

Klakke's cheeks grew pink. "I . . . I . . . I was feeling a little neglected. I didn't get my rice pudding on Christmas Eve."

Ulf ignored his young cousin's confession and

continued. "And didn't I know too well the risks involved when one indulges in self-pity? I took care of the animals, then I left the barn and returned to the forest thinking perhaps I could convince Gammel to reinstate me to my post at the Larsens'."

Klakke's pink face became very pale. Even Bettina felt alarmed. Would Ulf really have gotten Klakke reassigned, simply because he'd been upset about his Christmas pudding?

"I wandered a bit in the winterfrost, trying to think of the right words. The longer I wandered, the more I doubted my plan. Were you and I really so different, Klakke? Hadn't I been doing the same thing when I neglected to check the latch on Kasper's stall? Sulking? The only difference between us, really, had been luck. Mine turned out to be much worse than yours.

"It was thinking of this bad luck that made me question my plan to reconcile with my father. Would he really welcome me now? Hadn't I proved to be an unreliable barn nisse by running off and hiding rather than facing my mistakes? I sat under a fern near the big oak for hours, losing my nerve, and wondering if I should just go back to Askø. And then you appeared, Klakke."

"With baby Pia."

"With Pia. When you set her down outside the door of the big oak and went inside, I couldn't believe my eyes. You had taken a human baby? Even worse, you had left her on the frosty ground all by herself? I knew I had to act quickly. It was the perfect opportunity. If I held on to the baby for just a day or two, I could return her safely to Gammel, say I'd found her in the forest—which was no lie—and I'd be the hero who saved the day. Surely Gammel would welcome me home then."

From the hearth, Klakke groaned and put his head into his hands. Bettina knew he must be regretting his impulsive decision to take Pia in the first place. She felt bad for the young nisse, yet at the same time she couldn't really blame Ulf for wanting to teach Klakke a lesson. He had been very foolish and wrong to take baby Pia, even though he'd meant her no harm.

"So I brought Pia here, and I've been taking very good care of her."

"But why haven't you returned her to us?" Bettina

asked, recalling Ulf's plan to keep Pia just for a day or two.

"I was ready to bring her, but before I could leave, my brother-in-law showed up."

Bettina had nearly forgotten that Hagen had paid Ulf a visit yesterday!

"Why didn't you give her to Hagen to bring home?" she asked.

Ulf looked at the wooden floorboards. "I wasn't happy to see Hagen. It was my father I really hoped to see, and the conversation didn't go well. He reminded me that by taking Pia, I'd only further damaged my relationship with the Larsen family. And that's why my father sent you, Bettina. He knew that there would be no mending the father-son relationship until I'd made everything right with you."

From the cradle came a soft, contented coo, and Pia's eyes fluttered. Klakke leaped to his feet at the sound.

"May I?" Bettina asked Ulf, her heart aching and Pia so close.

"Of course."

Bettina wasted no time scooping up her sister from

the bed. Still wrapped in the thistledown blanket, Pia was the softest, warmest, most wonderful thing Bettina had ever felt.

The little girl's sleepy eyes spotted her older sister, and she awakened more fully. She laughed and reached for Bettina's face. Bettina held her close.

"I'm sorry," Bettina told Ulf. "I'm so sorry for . . . for all you've been through. It's not fair that you've been made to suffer so much for a mistake. But I've been suffering too, with my sister missing." She took a cautious step closer to the door, trying to form the words in her head that would allow her to gracefully exit both the conversation and the house.

With Pia still snugly wrapped in her arms, Bettina made her wishes known.

"I would like to go now and take Pia home. My parents will be—"

Ulf raised a hand to stop her.

"No. First you must help me."

Bettina's excitement over finding Pia gave way to new fears. She held Pia a little closer.

"But I don't know how I can help you, Ulf. You've

got the forgiveness of the Larsen family, if that's what you need. I believe you didn't mean to harm Kasper, and I don't blame you for his death. Now, all I want is to get Pia back home."

"Listen to me, Bettina. In my own efforts to reconcile with my family, I've made things worse. I now have to answer for what happened to Kasper all those years ago, *and* I have to explain why I've been hiding a baby on Askø these past days!"

Ulf's frustration was unnerving. An old saying, a favorite of Farfar's, kept running through Bettina's mind. *You made your bed, now you must lie in it.* Ulf's actions had gotten him into this mess. He should have never taken Pia in the first place.

Still, how long should a person have to lie in the bed he'd made? Forever?

"But how can I help you?" Bettina asked, no matter that she wasn't sure if she even wanted to.

Ulf began to pace the dull wooden floor. With every step, his desperation grew more evident, until finally he stopped and made his wishes very clear.

"You must go to my father and tell him that we've

met, and that you've forgiven me for taking your sister from Klakke."

Bettina listened carefully.

"And then you will tell him that you believe me when I say that I didn't leave the horse stall unlatched on purpose. And that I didn't leave because of a guilty conscience, but because I couldn't bear watching someone else do the job I was born to do. And I couldn't bear my father's disappointment."

Bettina understood disappointing an elder. Though she had only disappointed Far a few times in her life, each instance was seared into her memory and caused her to prickle with shame to recall it. And now, with the clock ticking away precious hours until her parents returned, Bettina risked disappointing them in the most unthinkable way possible. She must get Pia home. And if helping Ulf was the only way to make that happen, she'd just have to do it.

"All right, then," Bettina agreed. "I will go to Gammel, and I will do what I can to help you return to your family, Ulf."

The corner of Ulf's mouth turned upward in the

smallest of smiles, and Bettina noticed for the first time a bit of the family resemblance. "Thank you, Bettina Larsen. Thank you!"

"I guess we'll be off, then," Bettina said, inching closer to the door. "Say good-bye, Pia!"

"Wait!" Ulf cried.

Bettina frowned. *What now?*

"You may go. But Pia must stay here."

"What?" Bettina couldn't believe her ears.

"Once you have your sister back home, what's to compel you to keep your word and speak to Gammel on my behalf?"

Bettina promised she would, but Ulf remained unconvinced.

"No," he said. "The child stays."

Bettina looked at the door and back to Ulf. She already had Pia in her arms. She could just go, make a run for it. But then what? There seemed to be no rhyme or reason to when or how she would return to her proper size. And if she left the house and remained small, transportation seemed to be another unknown. She simply could not take the baby out into that awful freezing rain until she was sure they could safely return to Lolland.

Then Bettina had an idea. "Pia may stay," she said, "only if Klakke stays, too."

Klakke's eyes widened. "B-but—" he sputtered.

"Klakke," she said, her tone pleading, "I know you best and trust you most. Please stay and be certain that Pia is well taken care of."

Klakke twisted his mouth from one side to another as if he was considering his options. Just then baby Pia stretched out a chubby hand toward the familiar nisse and smiled widely.

"OK," Klakke answered, smiling back at Pia.

Ulf frowned. Once again, Klakke had been chosen over him. Bettina waited for the nisse to accept her compromise.

"If that's how you want it . . ." he began.

"It's settled, then," Bettina interrupted. "I'll go alone and be back as soon as I can."

This seemed to amuse Klakke.

"Alone!" He laughed. "Haven't you learned that in the forests and fields, one is seldom alone?"

Promises

To say that Bettina was unhappy to be leaving Askø without Pia would have been an understatement. As she trekked from the forest to the tall, grassy fields, she wondered if she had done the right thing. But what choice had she had? Ulf was holding Pia as collateral. He'd trade Pia for his father's forgiveness, and it was up to Bettina to get it. At least Klakke was there. That single thought offered some comfort as she marched toward Askø's small harbor.

Bettina's problems only seemed to multiply as she walked. She had no idea how she would get back to

Lolland. Stowing away on the old green Askø ferry would have been an option, but at this size, the only way to get aboard would be to skim the ropes, which would mean dangling far above the icy waters. Bettina's small hands were already red and raw with cold. Could she trust them to hold on?

She knew that just before the ferry departed, the ferryman would let down the ramp for cars and people— if there were any of either this time of year—to enter. But scurrying across that ramp between giant wheels and heavy feet seemed just as dangerous as trying to board by rope.

Bettina was deep in thought when, behind her, something rustled in the dry leaves alongside the stone road. Bettina stopped. She listened. Nothing. She moved on only to hear the patter of small boots on the stones a moment later. Quickly she spun around, but behind her was just an empty lane.

Bettina decided to pick up her pace, nearly running. But the patter of feet was more evident than ever, and whoever was following her seemed to have no problems keeping up.

And then she heard a small voice.

"You'd make a good nisse—for honest," it said.

Bettina slowed to a walk again. "Hello?"

She looked left and then right, and when she turned to face forward once more, she saw before her a young female nisse.

"I know you're not actually a nisse, despite your size just now," the nisse said. "But you can move nearly as quickly as we move, so you'd make a good nisse."

"Thank you," Bettina said.

"You're welcome."

Bettina tried to look this nisse girl over without staring or seeming impolite. She was the size of most nisse, not so plump as Pernilla, and dressed more like the men. She wore red leggings, brown boots, and a long brown coat with thistledown lining. On her head, a pointed red cap sat neatly over two long blond braids that did resemble Pernilla's.

Bettina stuck out her hand and introduced herself.

"I know who you are," the young nisse said with a twinkle in her eye. "You've become quite famous among the Lolland nisse, Bettina Larsen."

"Are you from Lolland as well?" Bettina asked.

"I'm not, but I have family there," she said, without introducing herself. "And I'd love to travel with you back to Lolland, if you don't mind the company."

"I'd be delighted!" Bettina said. There was something wonderfully familiar about this new nisse, and Bettina felt as if they'd been friends for years.

Their short legs fell into stride with one another as they marched on.

"What are you doing on Askø?" Bettina asked after a time.

"Oh, a bit of this, a bit of that."

Bettina was more curious than ever, for what was there to do on a frozen island in the dead of winter? But it was clear that her companion didn't feel like sharing. "If you have family on Lolland, then perhaps you know Gammel," Bettina wondered aloud.

The little nisse giggled.

"Is that a silly question? Do you know a nisse woman named Pernilla? She has two young twins, Tika and Erik."

Again, the girl laughed but said nothing.

"What about Klakke? Have you met Klakke? I think you'd remember him if you had!"

At this, the nisse stopped walking, sat down on a large pebble, and laughed until she had to wipe the tears from her eyes.

"Of course, I've met Klakke!" she said, when she could speak at last.

Bettina studied the young nisse girl closely, wondering what was so funny. Suddenly, something struck her. "You know, you look a bit like Klakke. Are you Klara?"

"It took you long enough to figure it out."

Klara stood and hugged Bettina. "Forgive me, won't you? I should have introduced myself right off, I suppose, but I couldn't resist a bit of fun."

If Bettina had had any doubts that Klara was Klakke's sister, this bit of mischief would have dispelled them!

As the two moved closer to the Askø shoreline, Klara explained her real reasons for being on the island. Her parents had sent her from Falster to deliver to Klakke some clothing and treats their mother had made. But when she'd arrived at the Larsen farm, she didn't find her brother. Instead, she'd found a note about a stolen child and a journey to see Ulf. What crazy mess had Klakke gotten himself into now, she'd wondered.

"When I entered the forest, I spotted him just as he was about to go into the big clearing. I nearly shouted out to him when I saw he was being followed," Klara explained.

"I was following him!" said Bettina.

"Yes, it was you. And it looked like you might be gaining on Klakke, so I summoned a seagull as quickly as I could. I told the gull where Klakke wanted to go, and away he went!"

"*You* did that to your brother?" Bettina asked.

"I was only helping him out. It worked, didn't it?" Klara shrugged. "He'll thank me later."

"Then what?" Bettina asked.

"Then I followed you while you visited Gammel, and I arranged for the Pedersens' goose to pick you up, and then I came straight here on the next gull going north."

Bettina was amazed! It seemed Klara had all of Klakke's spunk and maybe a bit more common sense.

"I've been wondering something," Bettina confessed. "How do you suppose I'm — we're — going to get across the sea back to Lolland?"

Klara giggled. "Humans fuss over the silliest things!"

Sure enough, when they reached the shoreline, Klara turned away from the ferry and waved one arm high in the air, in a sweeping arch overhead.

"You, too," Klara instructed, and Bettina obeyed, swinging her own arm in a similar manner.

Very soon two seagulls swooped low. "You've got to be kidding," Bettina said.

She screamed and ducked, placing her hands over her head, fully expecting to be snatched up in a sharp, crooked beak. But one of the birds landed in front of Bettina, squawked once, and motioned toward his back with his large white head.

The bird squawked again and repeated the gesture.

Klara had already climbed atop her gray-and-white gull, which was running along the frozen-sand runway.

"Hurry up!" Klara called over her shoulder. "He'll leave without you!"

Bettina hoisted herself up, and the gull wasted no

time launching into flight. This bird lacked the soft padded seat that the Pedersens' fat goose had provided, and Bettina found the flight to be overall jerky and uncomfortable. Between that and the wind and rain, it was impossible for the girls to converse with each other while in flight.

Bettina closed her eyes and held on tight.

To his credit, the seagull was faster than the goose had been, and soon enough they were inland over the frosted Lolland forest, landing in the very clearing where Klakke had been snatched. If this was the same seagull that had taken Klakke, Bettina was grateful that she'd been transported in a gentler manner! Of course, she had no way of knowing, as one crooked-beaked seabird looked exactly like the next.

The girls waved good-bye to their waterfowl taxis and walked through the tall grasses toward the forest. Bettina was thrilled to see that the winterfrost lingered. Askø had been so dull and bare, but Lolland still sparkled with millions of iridescent flakes of frozen fog.

As Bettina walked, something strange began to happen. The tall brown grasses on either side of her grew shorter. With each step, Bettina's head rose higher above the ground, and she watched in amazement as her tiny booted feet grew larger. She was returning to her normal size. At last, when she could look across the horizon and see the fields of Lolland, she looked down at her companion.

Klara stood below, tinier than even Bettina guessed she would be. It was hard to believe Bettina herself had ever been so small.

Bettina frowned. She'd hoped to remain small until she'd had a chance to speak with Gammel and get back to Askø. One thing was certain. Her size was something over which she seemed to have no control these days. She could only hope that once she got to the door of the house beneath the oak, the old shrinking trick would work one more time.

"Don't look so disappointed," Klara called up to her. "We can still travel together."

So Bettina moved on and Klara dashed in a blur of red, sometimes staying with Bettina and sometimes passing her by.

At the forest's edge, Bettina became very aware

that evening was setting in. Thoughts of all that had occurred since she'd set out that morning after Klakke were dizzying. Could so much have really happened in one short day?

It felt good to be back in familiar territory, and, she had to admit, it felt good to be back to her usual size. She marveled at the enormous tracks her boots left on the snowy forest path, and though she didn't have the speed of Klara, she could cover a lot of ground in a single step.

Perhaps it was because she was looking down that she didn't see him coming. Perhaps it was because she had so much on her mind that it didn't occur to her that her neighbor Rasmus Pedersen might be out walking on the same forest path.

It didn't occur to her, that is, until she rounded a fat fir tree and ran smack-dab into him, her face smashed up against his scratchy wool coat.

Obstacles

"Well, look who's here!"

Mr. Pedersen grinned, looking genuinely happy to see his young neighbor. He extended his right hand to Bettina, who shook it politely, her mind racing as she anticipated his next question.

"You alone?" Sure enough, there it was.

"Yes," Bettina answered, knowing it was Pia her neighbor was referring to, but she was wondering if Klara would stay out of sight. "I left Pia napping at home while I . . ."

She hesitated. Why would she be out in the forest at dusk? She should be home making dinner. Of course, that was it!

"While I gathered winter greens for a salad. Do you know that fabulous winter greens are hidden beneath the snow, even in December? Why, there's chickweed, white nettle, cow parsley," she quoted from memory, proud of herself for remembering Hagen's every word.

"Well, I'm impressed." Mr. Pedersen nodded, though he looked at Bettina's empty hands a little suspiciously.

"I, um . . ." Bettina stammered. "I haven't had any luck yet."

Mr. Pedersen nodded. "I'm going to get on home. Mrs. Pedersen was cooking beef with onions when I left the house, and, oh my, did it smell fine!"

His face brightened with an idea. "Say, why don't you and Pia come over for dinner this evening? I'm sure Lisa's got plenty for all of us."

"Oh, thank you, Mr. Pedersen. It's so kind of you to ask."

Bettina could feel her heart pounding beneath her winter coat. Her scarf suddenly felt hot and itchy on her neck.

"I've actually got soup on the stove. I couldn't let it go to waste. And I really must get back to Pia now, before she wakes and finds herself alone. Good-bye, Mr. Pedersen. And thank you again for the invitation."

Bettina was already moving down the path away from her neighbor, talking as she did.

Mr. Pedersen turned to go. A few more steps and she would have been out of sight, but it seemed he had one more question for her.

"Bettina?"

She slowed. "Yes, sir?"

"You sure everything's OK at your place?"

Bettina turned and flashed the biggest smile. "Oh, yes. Good as can be." It wasn't really a lie, given the circumstances. "I'd best get home now. To Pia. And the soup. Tell Mrs. Pedersen I said hello!"

Before her neighbor could respond, Bettina dashed toward her house. She waited until Mr. Pedersen was out of sight before she doubled back and headed straight for the giant oak. Klara was nowhere to be seen, and Bettina was afraid to call out to her. Mr. Pedersen might still be in the woods and hear.

The sky had turned from dusky to a deep charcoal gray, and Bettina worried that she wouldn't be able to find the door under the root. But, sure enough, when she lay flat on her belly and moved the leaves aside, just enough light remained to find the little door. She lifted the knocker and let it fall.

There was a long silence. Bettina was deciding if she should knock again when the door opened and Gammel stepped outside. He was in his nightclothes and night-cap and held a rather large firefly, whose light filled the small space beneath the root outside the door with an intermittent golden glow.

"Bettina, my dear. I was hoping you'd stop in tonight. We were just rising for the evening."

The old nisse craned his neck and lifted his light to see behind Bettina. "Alone, are you?"

Bettina nodded. Had he expected to see Pia with her? Or someone else? She would have mentioned Klara, but perhaps Klara wouldn't want Gammel to know what she'd been up to. Where was the little nisse girl, any-way? Bettina had a feeling she wasn't far away.

"Well, then, do come inside and tell me of your journey."

Whooshing in and out of the nisse's world was becoming so common to Bettina, she hardly thought twice about it, but this time she declined.

"If you don't mind, could we talk out here?" Bettina knew if she went inside, she'd surely be offered a cup of Pernilla's sweet hot cider, and not long after, they'd offer a downy alcove and she'd be there until morning.

"Of course," Gammel agreed, pulling the door closed behind him. "Tell me. Did you find your sister and our Klakke with Ulf?"

"I did." Bettina told him all about their meeting in the wooded cottage on Askø. Gammel seemed genu-inely pleased to hear of Klakke's and Pia's safety, and he thanked Bettina for her part in Klakke's rescue from the tree. When she finished, there was a long pause. Gammel seemed lost in thought, and then he asked about Ulf.

Bettina didn't waste any time getting straight to the point. "Your son wants to come home."

"I see" was all he said.

Bettina went on. She explained Ulf's sadness over the loss of Kasper and how he hadn't meant to do anything wrong. She pleaded Ulf's case with passion, trying to convince Gammel that Ulf should come back. As she did, she realized she really did believe that he deserved a second chance.

Gammel stood very still while Bettina talked. In his long white gown and cap, he looked every bit of his 392 years. The firefly's light illuminated his face and highlighted the lines each smile and worry had left behind. Maybe Ulf was right. Maybe time was running out for this father and his son to reconcile their differences.

"I've forgiven Ulf for taking Pia from this tree," she said. "Just as I've forgiven Klakke for taking her from the patio. My farfar was a wonderful man—"

Gammel nodded. "I can attest to that."

"—and he taught me many things, but, most of all,

he taught me kindness. He would have forgiven Ulf for his part in what happened to poor Kasper. If he had known, he would have. I know it."

Gammel listened carefully to all Bettina had to say. When she was finished, she was sure she had won the old nisse's heart for his son. But when he spoke, her own heart nearly broke in two.

"I'm sorry, dear girl," Gammel said, his voice soft and apologetic, "but it is not your responsibility to come pleading on my son's behalf. Ulf should have returned your sister to you and come to me himself, to make amends. The greatest good comes when each takes responsibility for his own mistakes."

"Yes, I know, but—"

Gammel raised a hand to shush Bettina. "You've done what I asked of you, and you've done what Ulf asked of you. I'm sure he'll have no issue with returning Pia to you now. If you need my help returning to Askø in the morning, just let me know."

And with that, Gammel went inside and was gone.

By now the forest was completely dark. Bettina stood and looked toward home, frustrated and cold. How could Gammel be so stubborn? His remorseful son was ready to make amends, to end a twelve-year misunderstanding. Why couldn't he just accept Ulf's apology — even if it did come from a human? *He* was supposed to be the wise one, but Bettina felt sure she was the only one thinking rationally.

As much as she didn't want to admit it, Gammel was right about one thing: it was too late to return to Askø now. The night was black, and there didn't seem to be a goose or gull waiting to take her anywhere — not that one could while she was still human size, she reminded herself.

Bettina didn't need light to find her way now that she was back on familiar ground. She knew every tree, every bend in the path between the giant oak and home. She was just steps from the backyard when she began to feel as if she was no longer alone. She smiled to herself and continued walking. She listened most astutely to every crackle of twigs under her boots, every rustle of dead leaves as her coat sleeve brushed by bushes along the path, trying to detect any sounds from the nisse world. Then she stopped quickly, her body as frozen as the December air.

Swish, swish, swish.

"Klara?" Bettina called.

Silence.

"Klara, I heard you running," she said.

Then *swish, swish.* And a giggle.

The little nisse appeared.

"Oh, I was trying to stay hidden!" Klara's cheeks were pink — because of the night air or because of being spotted, Bettina wasn't sure. Red faced or not, she was a delightful sight to Bettina's weary eyes.

"So, how did it go? With Gammel?" Klara asked.

"You weren't there? I thought maybe you were lurking nearby."

"Nope. I had things to do. So? How'd it go?"

"Not so well," Bettina said. She filled Klara in on her conversation with Gammel as they followed the path through the woods that led to the Larsens' back garden. "I'm going to have to convince Ulf to come face his father himself," she concluded. "And I have no idea how."

"You'll think of something, Bettina. A good night's sleep in your own bed will do you good."

At the edge of the garden, Bettina stopped. "I can't sleep. There are chores to be done."

Klara giggled with excitement.

"Done!"

"Surely the fire must have gone out."

"Done!"

"Really?"

Klara skipped gleefully. "Done, done, done!" she chanted. "Klara has the speediest feet in all of Denmark!"

Bettina laughed. "And I am very grateful for it!"

In the kitchen window a welcoming light glowed, and in the barn the haymow light seeped through the crack in the big red doors.

"Won't you come inside with me?" Bettina offered, but Klara was already halfway to the barn.

"No," she answered. "I should like to be a house nisse

someday, but tonight I'm taking care of my brother's work. I'll see you when I see you."

Bettina waited until Klara had disappeared before she went into the warm house. As she showered and dressed for bed, she realized how much richer her life had become now that she believed in something Farfar had always known to be real.

But, oh, how empty was Bettina's heart without her baby sister! And how devastated her parents would be if they returned and—

Some thoughts are best left in the unthought corners of our minds. Most of them begin with *What if* . . .

Bettina fell asleep that night pushing all her *What if* . . . thoughts into the deepest corners she could find.

Plans

Bettina slept so well in her own bed, it surprised even her. She woke clear headed, and before she even left the warmth of her bed, she had formulated a plan. Well, most of a plan. There were a few small details to work out, but she hoped those would come to her in a timely manner.

When the sun crept up over the fjord, Bettina was dressed and ready to face the day. She knew that everything had to go right in order for the outcome to be perfect. The end of Far's week in Skagen was quickly approaching, and Mor and Mormor could return from Århus at any time. Several obstacles remained that could prevent Bettina from having Pia home in time, and she just could not let that happen!

Unfortunately, Bettina would have to face one of those obstacles early in the day. How, exactly, would she return to Askø? In her human-size state, she was quite sure there was not a single bird in all of Denmark big enough to do the job. No, she would have to arrange her own transportation, and she knew what that meant. With a sigh she felt halfway to her toes, Bettina took the tea tin from under her bed and emptied it into her backpack.

She dressed and ate a bowl of oats and milk so quickly, she really didn't taste them at all. Then she headed to the barn. Amazingly, the winterfrost still hung around, and Bettina couldn't help feeling that anything was possible when the world looked so magical.

There was no sign of Klara in the barn, but the chores had been done and the tools all hung in their proper places. In the corner by the door stood the family's bicycles, all of them unused since October. Bettina had to dust hers off a bit before opening the barn doors to wheel it out. No sooner was she out the door than she noticed the front tire. Flat as a pancake. Mor's bike, too, she discovered with dismay, had one flat tire. Far's bicycle was the only one in working condition, so she mounted it, her tiptoes barely touching the barn floor. Teetering precariously as she rode down the driveway, Bettina was finally on her way.

She knew the main roads would be free of snow, but the back roads might be a bit tricky. Sure enough, she ended up walking the bike more than riding it until she got to town. Then she pedaled furiously toward the fjord. It was early enough that she was able to glide past the closed shops without being noticed. She even managed to avoid the workers from the night shift leaving the sugar factory by ducking through an alley and out the long road toward the harbor.

Harbor traffic was sparse at such an hour, and Bettina was at the ferry and waiting, somewhat impatiently, ten minutes before the ferryman arrived for the day's first crossing.

"In a hurry to get to Askø?" he questioned with a

high-pitched cackle, then used his teeth to open a bottle of soda. Bettina was relieved that he didn't wait for an answer. Instead, he released the moorings and revved the engine of the green-and-white ferry boat.

"You're my first customer," he quipped. Bettina handed him the fifty-crown fare for one passenger with a bicycle. The ferryman nodded and smiled, and Bettina noticed one of his front teeth was missing. *Perhaps it's unwise to open soda bottles with your teeth,* she thought.

Much to Bettina's dismay, the ferryman waited five, ten, fifteen minutes for other passengers. When none came, he finally set the ferry in motion.

"Guess you're not just my first customer, but my only customer," he shouted over the roar of the engine as they shoved off toward Askø.

Bettina gave the man a polite smile but said nothing. Instead she leaned over the small ship's rail, watching the water rush by. In the summertime, she would see pancake-size jellyfish pulse their way through the water, but not in December. In December the same cold gray-green sea churned past the ferry again and again and again.

Time passed nearly as swiftly as the water beneath the boat, and in less than thirty minutes the ferry was docking on the Askø shore. *Crossing by seagull was even faster,* Bettina thought.

"You visiting someone? There's not much here in the winter months," the ferry operator said as Bettina wheeled the bicycle down the ramp toward land.

Bettina smiled. "What I need is here."

He shrugged and took a long swig of his soda. "Sure hope you're right."

Persuasion

Bettina pedaled quickly past the empty summerhouses and deserted farmers' markets toward the small patch of dense forest on the far side of the island. She recalled exactly the flight of the goose. North, a little east. Sure enough, her memory was keen, and she was amazed at how much ground she could cover on her bicycle. The empty fields flew right by her, and the dry grasses that were tall enough to hide her view of the landscape the day before were just short weeds blowing in the winter breeze today.

Bettina ditched Far's bicycle at the edge of the woods. She would never be able to ride it through the dense underbrush.

And then, another obstacle. Could she find Ulf's cottage with the pinecone-scale roof? Tucked so perfectly among the leaves and moss, Ulf's tiny house would be easy to miss. Even though Bettina knew exactly what to look for, every tree looked the same as the one beside it. She walked the small patch of forest several times, until she knew that she was retracing her steps. After what felt like a very long time, she saw the white-barked tree that had snagged Klakke the day before. She laughed with surprise when she noticed that the branch he'd dangled from yesterday, which had seemed perilously high off the ground, was one she would have to bend down to reach today.

From the white-barked tree, it was easy to retrace the path to the tiny cottage with the pinecone-scale shingles, tiny front door, and little iron knocker. Moments later it lay before her eyes, a masterful blend of nature and architecture.

This time Bettina had to lie down on her stomach,

just as she had done at Gammel's house, and lift the knocker. It fell with the smallest of taps against the little oak door. There was a long, terrifying pause in which a thousand thoughts went through Bettina's mind. *What if Ulf wouldn't answer? What if Ulf had left again, taking Pia someplace else?* Panic rose in Bettina's throat, making it difficult to breathe.

Then the door opened, and it didn't take long for Bettina to realize that her human size had both advantages and disadvantages. Ulf himself, who ultimately held the fate of her family in his hands, seemed far less intimidating to Bettina when she was so much larger than he. But in this state, she could never get back inside the house to snatch Pia and run, if it came to that.

Ulf didn't invite Bettina inside. Instead, he stood just outside the door, looking hopeful and more humble than the first time they'd met. Perhaps he realized it was Bettina who held the fate of *his* family in *her* hands.

"Did you speak to my father?" he asked. "Do I have his blessing to return to Lolland?"

Bettina knew of no easy way to break the news to Ulf.

"I did speak to Gammel, but I'm afraid he won't accept an apology unless it comes directly from you."

Ulf sat down on the mossy green carpet outside his front door.

"I should have known better." He sighed.

"I'm so sorry, Ulf," Bettina said. "I did my best."

"It's no use," Ulf cried. "I'll never be accepted by my family again."

Bettina was worried. She was worried about Ulf's despondent state of mind. And she was worried that since he hadn't gotten what he'd wanted, Ulf would see no reason to give Pia back.

As if he could read her thoughts, Ulf stood up. With one long, disappointed look at Bettina, he went into his house and closed the door behind him.

Bettina rested her head on her arm. Was this it? Would she be forced to leave Askø again without Pia? Oh, the very thought brought instant tears.

"Ulf!" Bettina called through the closed door. "Please!"

Bettina waited, frozen for what seemed like many long minutes. At last Ulf returned, with Klakke close behind, and in Ulf's arms was tiny baby Pia. And in Pia's mouth was a tiny yellow beet-sugar pacifier! Pia's sweet blue eyes grew round when she caught sight of her older sister. If Pia was startled by her sister's large size, she showed no signs of it.

Pia squealed, barely keeping the pacifier between her lips.

A little sound — half sob, half cheer — came from Bettina's throat. Oh, how she longed to hold her baby sister! Bettina extended her hands, a little uncertain about how she'd hold on to such a small and delicate being.

With Pia still in his arms, Ulf looked up at Bettina. His dark eyes no longer looked menacing. A small smile curved his lips, and for the second time, Bettina could see the family resemblance. As the smile grew, Gammel's twinkle and Pernilla's sweet dimples appeared.

"She's all yours," he told her.

Ulf lifted tiny Pia and placed her gently in Bettina's waiting hands. As he did, Pia quickly returned to normal size. Bettina teetered and caught her balance, not expecting the weight of the almost-one-year-old.

"Oh, Ulf!" She laughed, hugging Pia tight. "You should have told me that was going to happen!"

Ulf shrugged. Klakke cheered to see the sisters reunited, bouncing up and down in an involuntary dance of joy. His wrong was at last righted! There couldn't have been a happier nisse in all of Denmark.

And yet, at that moment, there was likely not a sadder nisse in all the world than Ulf.

"I will miss that little one," Ulf said. "You're free to go home now, you know. Back to Lolland and back to your family."

He was speaking as much to Klakke as he was to Bettina.

"Thank you, Ulf," Klakke said with a sincere nod toward his elder cousin. "Your blessing means the world to me."

It seemed the two had come to terms regarding the care of the Larsen family, and Bettina was relieved.

Ulf turned his back to go inside. There would be no happy reunions for him.

"Wait, Ulf," Bettina heard herself say.

Ulf turned, and Bettina shifted Pia onto her hip. My,

how big she seemed. Bettina had to remind herself once more that Pia's first birthday was just days away.

Bettina knelt down and held out her free hand, palm side up.

Ulf studied Bettina's hand for just a moment before he climbed into her palm and she lifted him until they were face-to-face.

She looked into his small dark eyes. "Only a few short days ago, my only knowledge of nisse came from the stories Farfar had told me and the Christmas decorations we hang each year. Then I met your family. What kindness they've shown me! Gammel is wise beyond his three hundred ninety-two years, Pernilla is as sweet as the day is long, and—"

It suddenly struck Bettina that Ulf had never even met Pernilla's adorable twins.

"Oh, Ulf! You have the most precious niece and nephew!"

Ulf nodded. "I know. Pernilla sent word. And I hear stories sometimes, from nisse on holiday in the summer months."

Bettina nearly burst with the notion of plump nisse women and round nisse men in bathing suits on the beach, but she remained serious, knowing that her words might reunite yet another incomplete family.

"Ulf, you must come back to Lolland with us. You have to talk to your father."

Ulf's face softened a bit. Was he thinking about his home beneath the crooked oak? The warm fire? Pernilla's winter vegetable stew bubbling on the stove?

"A wise old gentleman told me once, *'The greatest good comes when each takes responsibility for his own mistakes.'*"

Ulf smiled. "Your farfar was one of the wisest men I've ever known. Nisse or human."

"He was very wise," Bettina agreed. "But those words came from your father, Ulf. From Gammel."

Ulf's eyebrows rose in surprise, then lowered in deep contemplation. At last he spoke.

"Well," he said. "If you'll put me down, I'll get my coat and hat. We should be going."

"You're really coming?" Bettina asked.

Ulf nodded. "I've stayed away long enough. If my family will have me, it's time to return to Lolland."

Bettina pedaled Far's bicycle toward the ferry with Pia riding happily in the child carrier on the back and both Ulf and Klakke tucked safely in her backpack.

Odd how things work out, she thought. If she'd ridden her own bicycle or Mor's, she wouldn't have had a child seat for Pia.

Back home, Klara would have chuckled over Bettina's way of thinking. There was nothing odd about the two bicycles' flat tires. But nisse, of course, rarely seem to get credit where credit is due.

More Mischief

At the ferry, the gap-toothed ferryman sat with his feet propped on the railing, another green bottle of soda in his hand.

"Good day, missy. Back so soon? It'll be an hour before I shove off again."

"An hour?" Bettina slumped, resting her forearms on the bicycle's handlebars. Mor and Mormor could arrive home at any moment. Or they could be home already, walking through the empty house, calling for the girls.

The ferryman didn't move from his spot.

"Yup." He tipped his bottle toward a weathered sign and a large clock hanging on the side of the dock house. "Got to stay on schedule. Says right there, next ferry crossing is at four o'clock."

Suddenly, the ferry driver noticed Pia.

"Where'd ya get that kid?" he asked.

Bettina straightened up and tried not to look as panicked as she felt. How could she possibly explain this?

"Play dumb." The voice came from her backpack.

"What?" Bettina whispered.

"I said, 'Where'd ya get that kid?'" the ferryman repeated, looking even more suspicious.

"Play dumb," the voice repeated. It was Ulf. "You can do it."

Bettina wasn't sure if Ulf had just complimented or insulted her, but she felt confident she could handle the ferryman.

"*This* kid?" she asked.

"Don't see no other," the ferryman answered.

"Why, she came over on the ferry with me today. You remember."

The ferry operator took his feet down from the railing and sat up a little straighter. "She did not."

"Sure, she did," Bettina insisted. "You must not have seen her in her child seat."

The man's eyes narrowed. "But you only paid for the bicycle and one passenger."

Bettina faltered.

"The sign!" Klakke whispered from her backpack.

Of course! Bettina motioned to the sign that read FERRY SCHEDULE AND FARES. "That's because children under two years of age are free."

The man took off his hat, scratched his head, and put his hat back on. "I must be losing my mind."

Bettina whispered over her shoulder. "Thanks, you guys!"

"We're not done yet. Wait until you see this," came Ulf's hushed reply. "Ask him what time the ferry leaves."

"But I already . . ." Bettina's voice trailed off as her eyes found the clock. She grinned and asked, "Sir?"

"What now, missy?"

"How long until the ferry leaves again?"

"I told you," the man grumbled. "The next trip back to Lolland is at—"

The ferryman stared at the clock.

"Four o'clock. Which is right now. Where on earth did the last hour go?" He leaped to his feet, nearly spilling his soda. "Well, get on board, then. We've got to keep to the schedule."

Bettina could hardly contain the giggle that bubbled up inside her throat.

"Yes, sir," she agreed as she pedaled her bicycle with all its tiny cargo onto the boat. "Got to stick to the schedule."

The ferryman scratched his head once more, took one long look at the bottle of soda in his hand, and then dumped the remaining contents over the railing and into the sea below.

Reunion

Gammel, Pernilla, and Hagen were all waiting beneath the crooked oak as Bettina pushed her bicycle along the forest path with Pia in the child seat and Klakke and Ulf still in her backpack. How they had known she was coming Bettina wasn't certain, but she'd stopped questioning the endless mysteries of the nisse folk days ago.

"I don't know if I can do this." Ulf's voice wavered like that of a person standing atop a very high ski slope, ski tips hanging over the edge, with no place to go but plummeting down, down, down the hill.

"It will be fine," Bettina assured him. "Just be honest. And try to keep your temper under control."

She lifted Ulf from her backpack and placed him at the base of the old tree, where he faced his father for the first time in twelve years.

With shaking hands, Ulf removed his red cap. "It's been a very long time, and I know I should have come sooner."

"Oh, Ulf!" Pernilla, with her round red cheeks already wet with tears, moved toward her brother, but Gammel raised his hand to stop her.

"First, let's hear what he has to say, shall we?" he said firmly, reminding everyone that he was still the senior nisse, the one in charge.

Pernilla stepped back, her hands fiddling nervously with her apron strings. Hagen placed his arm gently across her shoulders.

All eyes were on Ulf as he continued. "I've come to say I'm sorry. I'm sorry for what happened to Farfar Larsen's beloved horse Kasper. I meant no harm that day, as I have never meant any harm to any animal of the farm or forest."

Gammel nodded. A small gesture of approval though it was, it seemed enough to give Ulf the courage to continue.

"But most of all, I am sorry for leaving. I should have stayed and accepted the consequences of my carelessness. But I was jealous of my cousin Klakke. And it caused me great pain to know someone so young and inexperienced would be given the work I'd done for so long. I feared I'd lost my place in the world forever.

"So, you see, I now know things I didn't understand twelve years ago. Farfar was an unusual human, a rare individual who had room in his heart to love his new granddaughter and still believe in and care about the nisse on his farm. I know this now because of Bettina. He's no longer here, but he passed on his keen awareness of the natural world to his granddaughter."

Bettina's eyes stung with the memory of Farfar and the truth of Ulf's words. Farfar loved the farm, the forest, and all the inhabitants of both. And although she hadn't fully understood it at the time, he had worked to instill the same respect in Bettina.

Ulf stood tall, not begging, not groveling. Just being honest.

"I'm sorry. And I'd like to come home."

All of Lolland—every tree, every creature, even Klakke—stood still and silent in the long moments that followed. All eyes were on Gammel, whose creased brow now showed every one of his 392 years. At long last, the old nisse's thick gray mustache curled into a smile.

Gammel said not a word, but spread his arms wide to welcome his wayward son home again. Ulf sprang into his father's arms. Pernilla, who could wait no longer, joined their embrace. Even Hagen was moved and wiped his eyes on a small handkerchief.

When the family hug was over, Gammel cleared his throat, perhaps holding back his own tears, and spoke to his son.

"I, too, have done and said some things that I deeply regret. I was quick to judge, both twelve years ago and recently, when Pia disappeared. I may have reacted too swiftly, too harshly at times, and I certainly stand before you guilty of being far too stubborn. All I've ever wished for is to have you home with us, Ulf. Welcome back, my boy. Welcome back."

Klakke let out a small delighted cheer and scrambled down Bettina's back, only to change his mind and clamber back up again.

Bettina turned to try and see what the little nisse was doing and was quite surprised when he wrapped his small, chubby arms as far as he could around her neck and squeezed. A fine nisse hug if ever there was one.

"Oh, Klakke!"

Klakke blushed, his always-rosy complexion turning as bright red as his nisse cap. He gave little Pia a quick kiss in her seat on the back of the bicycle, and both child and nisse giggled.

While Hagen, Pernilla, and Ulf disappeared beneath the oak tree's biggest root, talking among themselves, Gammel stayed behind and addressed Bettina.

"Won't you come inside? There is much catching up to do."

"No, thank you, Gammel. The catching up is for the family. Besides, I want to get Pia home."

Before anything else happens, Bettina added to herself,

glancing over her shoulder toward the house and barn-yard. As much as she adored the cozy little kitchen beneath the giant oak, she wanted more than anything to be home with Pia before anyone returned.

Gammel gave an understanding nod.

"What you have done, my child, we shall never for-get. You have not only reunited a broken family, but you have made great strides in maintaining the delicate rela-tionship between your world and ours. Together we can accomplish what we cannot do alone."

Bettina searched for words, but finding none that would do the moment justice, she just smiled.

Beneath his gray mustache and beard, Gammel's lips also spread into a wide grin, and his eyes twinkled behind his wire-rimmed glasses. Then he lifted a plump hand, waved, and disappeared beneath the root of the old oak.

"What about you, Klakke?" Bettina asked. "Are you going inside, too?"

"Oh, I'll come back later, after I've taken care of the chores at your farm. They need some time together. As a family, you know."

While Bettina was certain Klakke was happy about the way things had turned out, she detected a hint of melancholy in his voice. She remembered that Klakke was merely a cousin—a distant cousin from Falster— to Gammel's family. Perhaps he was feeling a bit lonely at the moment, but she knew just the thing to cheer him up.

Bettina opened her mouth to tell him not to worry about the chores, that Klara was looking after things at the farm. But she quickly closed it again. How much more fun would a surprise reunion be?

"OK, then," she said, turning the bike toward home. "Let's go!"

Klakke ran ahead, eager to get back to the barn and his own responsibilities.

Bettina sped up. "We've got to hurry!" she said to Pia. "We don't want to miss this!"

When the forest path ended at the Larsens' back-yard, Bettina lifted Pia from the child seat and leaned the bicycle against the barn.

Bettina opened the doors and carried Pia inside, but Klakke had already dashed through the crack between them. He darted right between Bettina's legs as she switched on the lights and revealed all the animals, eating contentedly and bedded down for the night. Klakke ran from the goats to the horses and back again. He checked the water buckets and stared in disbelief.

"This is terrible!" he cried at last.

"What's terrible, Klakke?" Bettina asked, faking concern. Above Klakke's head, high in the mow, she spied Klara, who waved and covered a giggle.

"The chores are done!" Klakke said. "This could only mean one thing. Your parents are home. Oh, Bettina, what are you going to tell them?"

Bettina smiled. She felt bad keeping her secret any longer. Just then, Pia tipped her head back and pointed high into the mow, babbling a long string of nonsense that only another almost-one-year-old would have understood.

All eyes turned upward, including Klakke's, which grew round when he spotted his sister standing on a bale of straw.

Klara let out a loud giggle and scurried down the ladder.

"Klara!" he cried. The two held hands and danced in circles in the most joyous of nisse celebrations.

"I thought it was time I paid my brother a visit," Klara explained. "And it turns out my timing was just right."

The young nisse girl winked at Bettina.

"Oh!" cried Klakke. "I should introduce you. Bettina, this is my twin sister—"

Klara and Bettina laughed so hard, Klakke stopped midsentence.

"You two have already met."

"Klara can tell you all about it, Klakke," Bettina said. "Right now, I need to get the house in order and get Pia to bed. Before my parents really do return!"

Klakke nodded in understanding. "Thank you, Bettina! This is the best surprise I've ever had in all my sixty-two years!"

Bettina turned to go, but then paused. "Will I see you again?"

Klakke looked thoughtful. "Do you believe I exist?"

After all that had happened, Bettina was surprised Klakke would ask.

"Of course! Sure as I am here, so are you!"

"Then, yes, I believe you will see me again," the young nisse answered. "But remember, whether or not you see me is not up to me. It is the seer who must do the looking, the seer who must slow down enough to take note of the world around her."

Bettina couldn't help but notice that Klakke sounded a little older, a bit wiser, perhaps. And could it be that a hint of gray was showing in his beard?

Bettina promised she would always take time to look carefully, and then she and Pia said good night to Klakke and Klara. A soft yellow moon was rising as the girls crossed the barnyard toward the house. Night was settling in across Lolland. The winter woodland animals were silent. Rabbits snuggled deep in their warrens, birds nestled in bushes for the night, and even the foxes were holed up in their dens. All of Denmark was enveloped in a hush so complete, Bettina could hear her own breath.

Just as Bettina reached for the doorknob, she felt a small breeze touch her cheek and the winter grasses around her shimmied ever so slightly. The smallest flakes of winterfrost fell to the ground. When she turned the knob and opened the door, a stronger gust swept over the garden, knocking more winterfrost from the bushes. By the time Bettina and Pia were safely inside the Larsens' kitchen, trees swayed and the whole farm was covered with falling frost. It looked like a gentle snow coming down.

Within minutes, the winterfrost was gone.

Home

Dawn in late December is gracious to those who long to linger beneath downy covers, peacefully dreaming even until breakfast time has come and gone. In the upstairs bedroom that the Larsen sisters shared in their family home on the island of Lolland, the morning sun didn't seep through the crack in the curtain until well past nine o'clock.

Bettina woke from the sweetest of slumbers, clear headed, not at all groggy, and hoping beyond all hopes that baby Pia was also sleeping, safe and sound, in her crib across the room.

And sure enough, baby Pia slept contentedly, with her stuffed goose beneath her chin. It was almost as if the past few days had been nothing but a dream. Bettina dressed quickly and was about to go downstairs to make tea when Pia began to stir.

"Hello, little girl!" Bettina greeted her sister.

Pia grinned, then yawned and rubbed a chubby hand over her eyes.

Bettina lifted her sister from her bed and carried her down the curvy, narrow stairs. As they descended into the kitchen, Pia let loose a string of babble complete with wide eyes and frequent gestures. Bettina understood not a single word.

"What on earth has you so excited, Pia?" Bettina asked. Pia, of course, could say nothing of the little nisse girl she'd seen zip past them on the staircase. And if Bettina hadn't been talking to her sister, she might have heard a soft but familiar giggle coming from the landing above.

"Oh, Pia, if only you could really talk! What a story you would have to tell."

But even as she said it, Bettina decided it was

probably best that Pia couldn't share all that had happened in days past.

Days past. How many days *had* passed since Bettina first opened the wood-room door and discovered the winterfrost?

From the kitchen window, the morning sun peeked out from behind a few sparse gray clouds on the horizon. Some snow remained on the ground, but the black tree trunks stood stark and bare, and the grasses looked brown and plain against the snow behind.

There was no sign that the winterfrost had ever been there.

With Pia securely in her high chair, Bettina toasted bread and spread Mor's raspberry jam over each warm and crispy slice. The teakettle sang as Bettina poured milk into Pia's sippy cup.

The kitchen felt warm and cozy, and as the girls enjoyed their breakfast, Bettina's gaze fell toward the place where the garden met the forest's edge. The forest didn't look so dark this morning, with bits and pieces of sunlight filtering in through the bare trees.

She wondered how the nisse family reunion was

going in the house beneath the big oak tree. She pictured the nisse talking late into the night over Pernilla's delicious cider, then retiring to their alcoves at sunrise with plenty of deep yawns and warm hugs to go around.

With one last glance at the forest, Bettina lifted Pia from the high chair and set her down to play on the kitchen floor.

Bettina gathered the breakfast dishes and filled the sink with warm, bubbly water. Meanwhile, Pia crawled to a kitchen chair, which she used to pull herself to her feet. When Bettina turned around again, Pia was standing alone, arms out and ready to catch herself if she fell.

"Pia," Bettina said softly, as if the very sound of her voice might interrupt the child's delicate balancing act. "Come."

Bettina squatted and held her hands out toward her baby sister. She held her breath as Pia lifted one wobbly foot and put it down again. The little girl, face tense with concentration, repeated the motion, propelling herself slowly across the kitchen. Each step nearly resulted in a tumble, but somehow the child managed to recover her balance just in time.

By the time Pia reached her sister's waiting arms, Bettina was laughing and crying and praising her little sister all at once. Pia beamed with excitement as she wiggled free to try it all once more.

The Larsen sisters spent the remainder of their time alone together feeding the animals, playing with new Christmas toys, and practicing walking all over the house. Mor and Mormor were on their way back to Lolland, and Far was close behind. It would be a grand surprise for all to see how baby Pia had changed while they were away.

But Pia wasn't the only one who had changed. Bettina never searched for winter greens without thinking of the cozy kitchen beneath the giant oak tree. She never once walked the forest trails without hearing Gammel's voice in her mind and remembering the night she accompanied him as he made his rounds among the forest animals.

Bettina's love for Christmastime returned. Farfar would never again be there to share in the holiday festivities, she knew, but his joy and excitement would remain as long as she kept them alive. Who else would tell Pia about the magic of winterfrost and the nisse of the farm and forest?

But most of all, Bettina never again went about her business in such a great hurry that she didn't take time to look. It is the seer, after all, who must slow down enough to take note of the world around her.

And though it didn't happen every day, or even every year, sometimes when Bettina was paying very close attention, she'd catch a glimpse of red as she walked through the pines or while she did her chores or rode her chestnut mare along the country roads.

And if she stood very still, and hoped and waited and believed, she would sometimes see a tiny nisse man, with a beard growing ever grayer with each passing year, stop and remove his hat and tip his head in her direction. Just to let her know that all was right between his world and hers.

Acknowledgments

I will forever be indebted to the families Poulsen, Christiansen, Højmark, Pedersen, Skammelsen, and Vestergård, who opened their homes and hearts to a young American stranger all those years ago; Danish children (young and old) who told their nisse tales to me via letter, e-mail, and mormor; all the Mainely Writers, especially those who accepted the challenge to read entire drafts of *Winterfrost*: Ann Mack, Nancy Roe Pimm, Thea Gammans, and Naomi Kinsman Downing; Laura Ruby for giving *Winterfrost* Uncle Viggo; Kaylan Adair and the incredible Candlewick team for believing in nisse; Karen Grencik for believing in me; Dora McAfee for her resourcefulness and generosity; Mark, Olivia, Seth, and Maggie for always saying, "We gnome you can do it!"; and the real Bettina, a tireless fact-checker and dear friend.